COWBOY CHARADE
Cowboys of Wildcat Creek, Book Six

BARBARA MCMAHON

1

Tyler Fallon pulled his pickup truck onto the large field behind the fairgrounds and bumped over the rough ground heading for his horse trailer. Pickup trucks and horse trailers were parked haphazardly everywhere, taking up almost the entire field. He saw one or two men stare as he drove in and he tightened his jaw in frustration and anger. He needed to feed and water the horses or he'd never have left Kyle behind.

Anger roiling, he banged the steering wheel with his fist. No matter what they'd argued all afternoon, the sheriff hadn't budged one iota. He found drugs in Kyle's pickup and was convinced Kyle was trafficking in drugs.

As if.

Kyle hardly drank--he'd never do anything like

use or sell drugs.

But the single-minded sheriff was convinced he'd caught a major criminal. No bail. Since it was Saturday, there was no arraignment until Monday morning. Kyle had to stay in jail another two nights unless something changed.

Like the sheriff continued to investigate until he found the real criminal who had hidden drugs in the door panel of Kyle's pickup.

And that could be anyone.

Tyler's headlights slashed through the darkness. With his windows open he could hear the muffled stomps of horses, the occasional outburst of laughter. Here and there small campfires illuminated the men sitting around them, swapping stories, bragging on their wins, ignoring losses.

Any other night and he and Kyle would have joined in.

He pulled in beside his rig and cut the engine. There was nothing he could do now but wait. And hope the sheriff would take some of their arguments to heart and at least give the appearance of searching further.

Tyler had heard rumors of drugs being sold at the rodeo, but he hadn't paid much attention. An athlete needed to keep on the top of his game to be competitive. This year was looking to be their best ever at team roping and bull dogging.

Except--they'd be out of the running if Kyle didn't get out soon. They'd already had to forfeit their entrance fees today. Tomorrow was the last day of the rodeo in Pueblo and then they were heading to Colorado Springs.

Only he'd be heading there alone if Kyle didn't make bail--or prove his innocence.

How did anyone prove innocence? Kyle didn't know the drugs were in the door. His finger prints would never be found on any of the bags of white powder that spilled out when that other car had run the red light and rammed the side of Kyle's pickup damaging the door and exposing the drugs.

Tyler pulled in behind his horse trailer and left the headlights on so he could see. He had to think of a way to get his partner out of jail and back on the circuit or the rest of the season would be a bust.

Jamming his cowboy hat on his head Tyler got out of the truck. First things first--he needed to tend to the horses—his and Kyle's.

His horses were still tethered to the side of the trailer where he'd left them. The buckets of water were full. Remnants of hay were scattered around.

"I fed and watered them. I didn't know when

you'd be back," a voice said from the darkness.

He looked over as a young woman accompanied by a large German Shepard stepped into the light from the truck.

He recognized her right away—Susannah Davis. They were following the same circuit so their paths crossed at every rodeo in Colorado. Tall and thin, she wore the standard jeans and cotton shirt, cowboy hat on her head. She always wore her blonde hair in a single braid down her back. She was one of the barrel racers who always placed in the top three–coming in number one more often than not this year. She had a sweet mare who could turn on a dime.

"Thanks. I wasn't sure either. Kyle's horse too?" Tyler asked.

"Yes. Where's your partner? All that came down the rumor mill was you two had been taken to the sheriff's office. When it got dark, I came to check on the horses."

He clenched his fists in frustration. "He's in jail for something he didn't do. And neither one of us can get the sheriff to listen to reason."

"Can he make bail?"

"It's not an option right now. He's considered a flight risk. Of course he's a risk, he doesn't live here. We're heading out tomorrow for Colorado Springs. Or we were."

"As a bunch of us are," she said. "What's he accused of?"

"Trafficking in drugs. Which is ludicrous. He's never touched the stuff, much less sold any. The sheriff won't listen. He's convinced he's arrested a dangerous criminal and plans to make an example of him to all rodeo cowboys that he won't tolerate drugs in his town."

She was silent for a moment.

Tyler wondered if she'd believe him or think what the sheriff thought.

"Does that mean you might have to pull out of the competition?" she asked.

"I hope not. But if I don't have a partner, I sure can't compete in team roping. Or bulldogging." Team roping required two, not a solo cowboy. And he needed a hazer for the steer wrestling.

He rubbed his hands over his face. He and Kyle had high rankings this year. Enough to think about the finals and the ultimate prize money. He could just punch something with the way things were going. Preferably the sheriff who wouldn't cut them a break.

This was shaping up to be their best year ever.

He and Kyle had been banking all the prize money they'd won over the last four years so they could buy a spread of their own. Winning at the nationals this year would have clenched it.

Now this. How did those blasted packets of drugs get into the truck door?

"Tough luck," she said. "Is there anything I can do?"

He looked at her. "Did you ever see any one around his truck– more than just hanging around? The drugs were in the door panel. A car ran a red light and smashed into the door. While the cops were investigating the accident, they discovered the drugs because of the damage to the driver's door. It doesn't take much to pop off the panel and then reattach with drugs inside the cavity."

She shook her head. "I'm not even sure I know which truck is his. All of us drive pickups. And a lot look alike. I guess cowboys all think black trucks are macho.

Tyler glanced at his own black pickup. "Maybe."

He didn't like her thinking he drove a black truck to appear macho. Did he?

She grinned. "I, on the other hand, drive a fire-engine red one."

"What statement are you making with that?" he asked, feeling his mood lighten slightly.

He'd known Susannah for a couple of years. Even asked her to a dance once last year. She explained she didn't date rodeo cowboys. That surprised him. But honoring her wishes, he never asked again.

"I've never really thought about it. Red's my favorite color, so that's what I picked when I bought the truck."

He glanced at the dog, sitting patiently at her side. The dog didn't wander far from his owner.

"That's why he's wearing a red collar?"

"That and I think red looks good with black and tan. Meet Radar."

Tyler nodded. "Do I shake hands?"

"You can with me. That way he knows you're a friend," she said with another grin and reached out to shake hands firmly.

"Glad he knows I'm a friend and not someone to attack. You're doing good this year. Heading for Las Vegas?"

"That's the hope."

"Yeah, we were, too. But if Kyle doesn't get out soon, that plan's a bust."

Tyler stepped closer to pet the dog. He was

surprised when his tail began to wag.

"He likes you. Nice. He's not always so friendly," Susannah said with a smile.

"That's smart of you to travel with a dog on the circuit. Some guys get a bit pushy when they've had too much to drink. Especially around pretty women."

"He's my best friend. He's a retired K-9. He was wounded and still walks with a limp so was mustered out, but he's perfect for me. I've got to go. Just wanted you to know I fed your horses."

"I appreciate it. If I can do something for you sometime, let me know."

"Will do. Good night."

Tyler watched her walk back into the darkness. There wasn't a thing he could do for his partner tonight. Checking on the horses again, he turned off the lights in the pickup truck. He walked the short distance to Kyle's trailer and checked his horses.

His thoughts were churning. How was he going to get his friend out of jail? And in time to continue on the circuit?

Susannah walked through the scattered horse trailers and pickup trucks on the field. Her own horse was in the make-shift corral near the row of stalls used for those spending a lot more money than she had. The mare ambled over when Susannah reached the fence.

"Just checking on you one more time," she said rubbing the velvety soft muzzle. "Be good. Tomorrow we have a shot at winning. Rest up."

Giving the horse one more pat, she and Radar headed for her pickup truck. She was sharing a room at a motel in town with Amanda Whitney. Some rodeos she slept in her truck, but she'd won more than a few times this season and occasionally splurged on a motel room. It was heavenly to have a hot shower and soft bed.

Who knew what she'd do on the next stop? Amanda wasn't going to Colorado Springs, she was skipping the next two on the circuit and would rejoin in Loveland later.

As Susannah drove into town she considered Tyler's situation. She'd been aware of him for a couple of years. He'd even asked her out once last year. Despite being tempted, she'd refused. She'd vowed after the Pete fiasco that she was not going to fall for another rodeo cowboy.

Once burned by a fun-loving cowboy, she was wary around men who had time to chase the dream.

If she ever fell for someone again, it would be a man who had a steady job, roots in one location, and the ability to be faithful to one woman.

Though how to gauge that before becoming involved was the big question.

Maybe someone who was faithful in other areas.

And loyal–like Tyler seemed to be.

Tyler was convinced Kyle was innocent. Yet, how did he explain the drugs in the truck? Could his friend be dealing without Tyler's knowledge?

Unlikely. From what she knew, Tyler and Kyle had been friends for years. Both came from some small town in Wyoming. Wildcat Creek she thought. Tyler would know his friend's values and obviously they were strong enough not to be involved with drugs.

She shivered slightly when she pulled her truck into the parking lot of the small motel. How awful that someone placed the drugs in Kyle's truck. If the sheriff didn't continue his investigation the true perpetrator could get off scot-free. If the truth didn't come out, his actions could cost an innocent man his freedom and reputation.

She turned off the engine and reached over to pet Radar. "You'll keep us safe, right, big fella?"

His tail thumped against the passenger-side door when he wagged it.

"Come on, let's get to bed. Tomorrow we ride, then pull out for Colorado Springs."

Lying in bed a short time later, Susannah tried to remember if she'd noticed anything out of the ordinary over the last couple of rodeos. Many of the same contestants followed the circuit, competing against each other over and over. Yet when not competing in an event, most cowboys were friendly to each other.

With a few exceptions. Devan Perlman came to mind. That cowboy had a chip on his shoulder that didn't quit. Quick to anger, itching for a fight every day, he was one cowboy she stayed clear of.

Though he had other ideas, it seemed. He'd asked her out a couple of times. She'd always refused and that hadn't set well with the cowboy.

She'd seen him knock down another rider just for the fun of it. She had no intention of going out with him and tried to stay clear of him. She could picture him thinking laws didn't exist for him.

Another exception was Juan Alvarez. That man gave her the creeps. His event was bronc riding, and he was good. But something about him seemed off to her.

Still, she didn't have anything but her dislike to suspect either man of being involved in drug trafficking.

Not that she knew what a drug trafficker looked like. If he was any good, no one would suspect–especially if he was using other people's trucks to transport the drugs.

Rolling over, she tried to sleep, but face after face of those men whom she saw over and over came to mind. Rodeo was a sport of the west. One that had been around for decades, starting in the old cowboy trail camps and rail heads where men from different ranches showed off their skills and the best of them claimed bragging rights.

She couldn't imagine anyone she knew tarnishing that legacy with criminal activities.

The last face she envisioned was Tyler Fallon's. He was one mighty fine looking man. And super handy with a rope. He and Kyle competed in the calf roping events, team roping and steer wrestling--and Tyler was the crazy fool who leaped off a running horse to wrestle an 800 pound steer to the ground.

He had the muscles to show for it. He almost had her thinking thoughts of a future–except he met none of her criteria. He sure didn't have roots to one place or a steady job. The faithfulness was up in the air, too. She'd seen him with a different woman in every town.

He wasn't for her. Eye candy, maybe. And that would be her limit. Admire from afar, but stay clear.

2

Tyler rode his horse in a tight circle, gradually widening as the gelding loosened up. He'd paid his entry fee for calf roping and he'd follow through with that event. The steer wrestling would have to be forfeited unless he got a hazer to work with him. Team roping was definitely off the table today.

He'd asked Jason Nichols to haze, but the man turned him down flat. From what he didn't say, Tyler suspected Jason wasn't convinced of Kyle's innocence. He acted like Tyler was a co-conspirator.

Tyler needed the hazer for that event since it didn't look like the sheriff was going to let Kyle out. Tyler had called the jail this morning to request Kyle be released for the rodeo events and be watched by a deputy. No go, according to the sheriff.

He took a deep breath. Getting riled up about

it again wasn't going to give him the focus he needed to win today. Once his events were over, he was heading to town to talk to the sheriff again.

Susannah rode up and stopped at the edge of the small exercise yard. Her dog was beside her horse.

"Mind if I ride?" she called.

"Come ahead," he replied.

She urged her horse forward and they began the circle at a walk, soon moving to the trot and then the lope. The dog lay down at the edge, out of the way and watched her as she rode.

He admired how she sat on the horse, moving together as if they were one. Gracefully moving with the horse, she was focused on the different gaits.

Tyler began again, keeping to the opposite side of the ring as he put his horse through his paces.

When she stopped, he continued until he was next to her, pulling his mount to a stop.

"Done?" he asked.

"I want the kinks out, but I want her to still be full of energy to perform her best," Susannah said, petting the mare on her neck. "You finished?"

"Yeah. I've done all four horses. I only need this one today for the calf roping."

"Couldn't you get anyone for steer wrestling? I know team roping's pretty specialized, but a hazer just rides in a straight line."

He looked beyond the fence to where contestants were milling around, some walking their horses, some grooming them, others leaning against the sides of trucks and trailers shooting the breeze.

"Seems some folks think Kyle might be guilty— and me, too, by association."

"I'm sorry. That sucks."

"It is what it is. But the sooner I can find the real culprit the better we'll all be."

"And how are you going to do that?" she asked, intrigued.

He glanced at her. Her blonde hair was in the usual braid down her back, her cowboy hat pulled low to shelter her eyes from the early morning sun. She was as pretty as a picture. He'd watched her in those barrel races for the last couple of years. Why hadn't he made a move to get to know her before this? She'd refused a date. But he could have spent some time with her without any involvement of a romantic nature.

He shook his head. He sure didn't have time for any thoughts like that. He had his partner to get out of jail and hopefully a buckle to win at the nationals.

"I haven't a clue. But the sheriff isn't looking any further. He's convinced he has the man responsible," Tyler said.

"I gave it a lot of thought last night," she said slowly. "There're a couple of guys I wouldn't mind being guilty, but I've never seen anything suspicious. Could it be someone not associated with the rodeo?"

He shrugged. "Who knows? It seems logical that the most likely guy is someone everyone's used to seeing so not to cause comment if he's around the trucks. And for all I know there're other trucks carrying drugs, too. It was Kyle's bad luck to have his in that crash."

She shook her head. "It's unlikely there's much more around," she said. "I mean, first of all there's the problem of finding trucks where no one sees him putting in the drugs. And then there's Radar."

"How's that?"

"Radar was in drug enforcement before he was injured. He gives a definite signal if there are drugs around."

"Did he ever come near Kyle's truck?"

"I have no idea, but if he did and there were drugs present, he would have alerted."

"So maybe the drugs were stashed there

recently," Tyler said thoughtfully. "That's the thing, we don't know if the drugs have been there for a day or two or weeks. If it's someone on the circuit, they could have stashed it there weeks ago, waiting however long they wants before opening up the truck door and taking them. Of course he'd have to make sure no one was around."

"I could walk Radar around before everyone leaves, just to see if anything suspicious pops up," she suggested.

"It'd be interesting to see if there's more. Or if this was their only stash."

"As soon as my event's over, we'll wander around," she said, urging her horse forward.

Tyler watched her, wondering what he'd do if Radar found more drugs. Should he call the sheriff right away?

Or should he wait until he had more to go on?

The announcement over the loud speaker ended his thinking. He had an event to win.

Tyler rarely watched the other events, focusing on his own events and psyching himself up to perform his best.

The one exception was the barrel racing. He liked watching Susannah perform. The ladies competing were good. He couldn't help think that

Susannah's form was the best and when she raced across the finish line, he didn't need the final score to know she'd won the event.

Now it was time for him to do likewise on his event. With only one event of the three he'd paid to enter, he needed a win to recoup the money from the entry fees.

When the calf roping event was up, he drew number seven. He hoped it would prove a lucky number. Though this was more a test of skill than luck. First lasso the calf. Then flip him on the ground and tie three legs, step back and pray the tie held.

Sonny was the gelding he used for this event and he was well-trained. In the off season, Kyle and Tyler kept up the training for all their horses. Sonny knew to pull the rope taut and hold until Tyler gave him the command to give it some slack. If the calf didn't rise in six seconds, it would all come down to time it took to put him on the ground.

Tyler knew he was good, but so were a lot of the other cowboys competing.

It was hot, and the sun blazed down from a cloudless sky. The arena was almost full. Sunday was the last day of this rodeo and the fans had turned out.

He loved the anticipation that was almost palpable at the beginning of each ride. The applause was often the only reward a rider had—especially if he ended up with a no time.

He sat on his horse outside the arena enjoying the few moments before he was up. The exhibit barns were to the far right. People were walking through to see the bulls and calves up for sale, the 4-H show stock. To the right, behind the arena were the holding pens for the rodeo stock.

Dust filled the air. A slight breeze kept it from being too hot to ride.

Another cowboy came out of the arena and nodded to Tyler. He was up.

Tyler rode hard, got the calf on the ground first try and tied the legs, stepping back, Sonny gave slack. The calf struggled to get to its feet but when the bell sounded, he was still firmly on the ground.

The crowd roared. Tyler waved his appreciation before stepping in to release the calf. He glanced at the scoreboard. His time was the best of the day. But there were six more cowboys before the event was over.

He wouldn't count on anything until the final score was posted.

He mounted Sonny and they rode slowly out of

the arena as he recoiled his rope.

Susannah was by the gate. She gave him a bright smile.

"Good job, cowboy!"

"Thanks. You did pretty good yourself."

He dismounted and moved out of the way of the next contestant ready to enter the arena.

She nodded. I'm ready to head out for Colorado Springs. How about you?"

"I was planning to. I need to check on Kyle first. If he can't get out, I need to see to his horses before I go. My rig's only set up for two and those are mine. I can't carry his, as well."

"Good luck. I hope they find the real culprit. I'll see you in Colorado Springs, then. Good luck with the event, I see you're at the top right now. Only a few more riders to go."

"Fingers crossed."

She gave him a bright smile and turned toward the field where the trucks and trailers were parked. Stopping suddenly, she turned back to Tyler.

"Oh, we walked around. Nothing."

"Thanks."

Tyler watched her walk away, liking the way she moved. Her braid swayed in the back. He wondered how long her hair was when not confined. Would it feel like silk or thick honey?

Sonny nudged him and Tyler turned to his horse.

"You're right, I'm crazy in the head thinking about silky hair when Kyle's stuck in some two-bit jail. Come on, let's get you settled so I can get into town."

Susannah had groomed her mare after her event. She collected her winnings and had packed everything up. Impulse had her going back to the arena to watch the calf roping event. She rooted for Tyler but kept her mouth shut in the midst of the others watching from the gate. He made calf roping look easy.

She'd tried it a time or two and came away chagrined she hadn't been able to lasso a single horn.

"Okay, Radar, we're ready to roll," she said, shutting the cargo door on the horse trailer after putting her saddle inside. "We'll make Colorado Springs before dark."

She needed to hitch the trailer to her truck and they'd be off. Some of the others had already left. The field was beginning to look empty. By the end of today's rodeo, it would be vacant again until the next time a rodeo played this town.

Suddenly Radar sank down on his belly and looked at her truck.

"What's up?" she asked walking to the truck. "Come on, it's time to move."

The dog didn't budge.

Susannah stared at him. His gaze was fixed on her truck, his ears alert, his gaze never wavering.

A sick feeling came over her. Slowly she opened the truck. Nothing looked disturbed. She saw her duffel bag behind the seats, some miscellaneous things she packed around it. The front seat was empty. She looked at the door. Wasn't that where Tyler said they'd found the drugs on Kyle's truck.

Closing the door, she walked over to Radar and squatted down beside him.

"Good boy. We'll look into it. Come on, I need to get help."

Only she wasn't sure which way to turn. What if she told the cops and they thought she was spooked by Kyle's arrest and a part of it--trying to avoid arrest if discovered?

Or what if the drug dealer was watching her to see what she did? What if he came after her or her animals?

Feeling really shaky, she headed over to where Tyler was grooming his horse.

"Tyler," she said.

He looked at her. "What's wrong?" he asked, dropping the brush and crossing over to her.

"Radar did his thing."

"What thing?"

"Alerting for drugs. And it's for my truck."

Tyler glanced around. "Are you sure?"

"I'm sure he alerted for it. I checked my truck and it looks okay, but what if there are drugs in the door like with Kyle? What should I do?"

"Let me get my horse settled, then you and I are going somewhere away from here to check it out. Okay?"

She nodded. "He could be wrong. He's been with me for two years now and only once alerted. Kids had some dope. Why would anyone put drugs in my truck?"

"Why would they put it in Kyle's? Risk-free transportation. Once we're where they want the drugs, they go in and remove it and probably no one's the wiser. Who knows–this could have been going on for months."

"Should we go to the police?" she asked.

He nodded. "Probably. But let's see what we

have if anything. The sheriff isn't the friendliest guy to rodeo cowboys."

"You don't think he'd believe I was transporting drugs?"

"Might not if you turn it in. But you never know. Maybe it's nothing. Maybe someone using drugs leaned against your truck at some point and that's what Radar's smelling."

She looked around, worry etching her face.

"Don't do that. Come on, let's go for a ride," Tyler said, brushing his fingertips across her forehead as if the erase the lines.

"What?"

"You have some tools in the truck, right?" He never knew any cowboy not to travel with tools to keep the rigs going.

"Yes."

"Okay, then we'll take your truck somewhere safe and check it out."

Radar reached Susannah's truck before they did. Once again, he lay down with his full focus on the truck.

"I'll drive," Tyler said.

Susannah handed him her keys and went to the passenger side and opening the door.

"Are we going to the sheriff's?" she asked,

snapping her fingers. Radar rose and jumped into the truck, over into the space behind the seats, settling on the duffel bag. She climbed in and slammed the door.

"Not yet. Let's check it out first."

Tyler glanced around. Not seeing anyone who appeared to be paying special attention to them, he started the truck. In only a couple of minutes, he turned left out of the field onto the road that paralleled the county fairgrounds. After about a mile, he turned right, keeping a close watch in the rear view mirror.

"Is someone following us?" she asked, turning around to look out the back window.

"Not as far as I can tell," he said, speeding up a little.

Two more turns convinced him no one was behind them. He then turned and headed away from town.

"Where are we going?"

"There's a rest stop not too far. Pretty isolated and run down. I don't think it's used much being so close to town. I figured we could stop there and see what's what. I trust your dog, but let's make sure before we try to figure things out."

Susannah nodded, glancing behind them one

more time. "Okay. I have to tell you I don't like this at all."

Tyler glanced at her. "No one does."

In less than ten minutes, he pulled off the county road into an overgrown rest stop. There were two wooden picnic tables to the left of the weed choked parking area. A dilapidated outhouse sat at the opposite end of cleared space.

Susannah wrinkled her nose. "Ugh, I can see why no one stops here. It looks awful."

"And isolated."

He pulled the truck as close to one of the picnic tables as he could. It was sheltered from view of the road by some wild brush overgrown and scraggly.

He got out of the truck and left the door open. In two seconds, Susannah was beside him, studying the interior panel of the door.

"I don't even know how to get it off," she commented looking at it.

"I can figure it out," Tyler said.

The dog jumped on the seat and almost knocked Tyler over when he jumped down to the ground. Turning, he lay down, his ears pricked forward at he stared at the door.

"He's alerting again," she said, glancing between Radar and the door.

Tyler rummaged in the space behind the seats and pulled out two screwdrivers. Setting to work, he removed screws, popped grommets and soon had the interior panel in his hands. Tucked into the spaces between the frame of the door were several plastic wrapped bricks of a white substance.

3

Radar never moved.

"Cocaine do you think?" she asked, reaching out.

"Don't touch anything," he warned, grabbing her hand and holding it away from the packets. "You definitely don't want a single fingerprint on the wrappers. That's one of the things I think will help Kyle. His prints aren't on the packets."

"Who would do such a thing?" Susannah asked, studying the packets carefully arranged around the framework. "Do you think the other door has stuff, too?"

"Don't know. But as Radar didn't focus on that door, I think this is the only stash." Tyler released her hand and lifted the panel back in place.

"What do we do now?" she asked as he carefully

reattached it to the door.

"Since I don't trust the way the sheriff works here, I suggest we call in help."

"Who, DEA?"

"Do you know anyone in the DEA?" he asked, finishing up and tossing the screwdrivers back into the truck.

"No, why would I?"

He shrugged, "I just wondered. I'm thinking more along the lines of a private investigator. Someone with a vested interest in seeing this kind of thing stopped, while protecting the reputation of the rodeo."

She looked at him, suddenly glad he was with her. She didn't have a clue how to handle the situation.

"And who is that?" she asked.

"Jesse Knight."

"I know that name. Wasn't he a championship bull rider a while back? I don't know him personally, but I've seen him ride. What could he do?"

"He and his brothers are connected to the rodeo. As I heard it they busted open a ring that was injuring animals and found they liked undercover work, so they opened a private investigation agency—primarily for situations involving rodeos.

The last thing any of us want is for authorities to shut down the circuit while the cops investigate."

"Which could take months."

"And maybe never turn up the perpetrators. They'll go to ground if they get wind of an investigation. Which is why Jesse would be perfect. He has ties to the rodeo and the knowledge to investigate what's going on without raising suspicions."

She rubbed her palms against her jeans. "Can't we take the drugs out and leave them here? No one would find them and I don't like driving around with them in the truck. What if I get stopped like Kyle did?"

"For the time being, let's leave things as they are."

He pulled his cell phone from his pocket and checked it.

"No service this far out of town. I'll track down Jesse and give him a call once we get back. In the meantime, act normally. You're heading out today, right?"

She nodded. "I was about ready to hitch up the trailer when Radar alerted."

"Hook up your trailer as normal and go. Don't get into any accidents."

She tried to smile but couldn't.

"Who would do this?" she asked again.

"I don't know, but we'll see if we can find out."

"Your truck's not transporting, right?" she said.

"You dog doesn't seem to think so, thankfully. Plus, the cops checked it while I was being questioned. I guess they figured Kyle and I were partners in more than team roping."

"This could ruin him and it's not his fault," she said slowly.

"I know."

"And me, too, if anyone finds this."

"Let's get going. The sooner we have some help, the better," Tyler said.

The drive back to the fairgrounds was quiet. Tyler reviewed what he knew about the Knight brothers. He'd met Jesse a time or two back when he was competing. How many people knew what happened then? Would anyone involved in drug smuggling know Jesse and his brothers had formed an investigation team?

If not, who better to be on the spot and able to keep an eye on things without arousing suspicion? He was willing to take that chance.

"You know, when we're all competing, the parking area's totally empty. Cowboys are either practicing or watching. Even the women competing like to watch the different events. Someone could easily put stuff in a bunch of trucks and no one ever see them," Susannah said.

"Let's just hope the sheriff doesn't come to that conclusion and start opening up every truck on the lot."

"Oh, I never thought of that. I want to leave right away."

"I'll help you hitch your trailer up and you can leave as soon as we get back. And I'd suggest not stopping until you are well away from town."

When they pulled into the lot, there were two county sheriff cars parked near the entrance to the parking area.

"Oh no," she said.

Her heart sank. What if they opened every truck door and found the drugs in hers. They should have hidden the packets at that rest stop.

"Don't borrow trouble until we know what's going on," Tyler said.

Two men in khaki uniforms were talking to a group of cowboys.

"Looks like they're questioning people," Tyler said.

He maneuvered her truck to her trailer, backing

up so it was ready to hitch.

"Act normal. Don't call attention to yourself," he said when he stopped the truck.

"I'm totally freaked and you want me to act normally." She took a shaky breath.

"You can do it," Tyler said.

When Susannah got out of the car Devan Perlman sauntered over.

He touched the rim of his hat.

"Susannah. Need any help?" he asked, giving Tyler a glance.

"No, I'm fine," she said.

He looked at Tyler.

"You two have something going on?"

Tyler grinned slowly. "And if we do?"

Devan scowled and turned away.

Susannah came around the back of the truck and frowned at Tyler.

"You let him think we're a couple."

"I wondered what he was doing coming over to check out the truck. Does he do that often?"

"This is the first time. He's one I wouldn't put it past to be involved. But he's also been hitting on me for weeks which I don't like, so I could be biased."

"So maybe we do act like a couple. Might keep

him away," Tyler said as he turned to get the hitch of the trailer lined up.

Susannah watched without saying anything. Despite his asking her out last year, would anyone believe Tyler Fallon would fall for her?

She didn't have a lot of confidence in dealing with the opposite sex. They'd been on the circuit for weeks and he'd rarely spoken with her before she fed his horses.

"That way we could stay connected with the case," she said slowly.

"Case?" he asked, looking at her.

"You know, find out who's doing this."

"You stay out of it," he warned.

"Like you're going to?" she retorted

"That's different. My partner was wrongly accused. I'm getting him out if it's the last thing I do."

"Mmm. So if I get busted, you'd get me out?"

He stepped closer and lifted her chin with his finger. Gazing into her pretty blue eyes, he slowly shook his head.

"You aren't getting busted. We'll figure this out. But don't do anything that would put you in danger. My guess is these drugs are worth a lot of money. And to some people, money counts more than collateral damage."

"We'll figure this out," she said with satisfaction.

"We as in Jesse Knight and me."

She stepped back out of reach and tilted her chin defiantly.

"I'm involved and whether or not you like it. I'll stay involved until I find out who's trying to use me to move illegal drugs."

"Okay, okay, keep your voice down," he said, glancing around.

The two sheriff deputies were walking their way.

"Heads up," he said softly, "I think we're next on the list of those being questioned."

"I thought they asked you everything yesterday," she said softly moving to help fasten the chain on the hitch.

As soon as the trailer was secure, she'd load up her mare and head as far from Pueblo as she could get in the next bit of time–without breaking any speed laws.

"Some deputies did. I don't recognize these two, however," he said.

He finished the last coupling and straightened.

"Do you have a minute?" one of the uniformed

officers asked as he and his partner stopped near them.

"What's up?" Susannah asked.

Her heart pounded like crazy. She hoped it didn't show. She was thankful Radar was still in the car. Even if they didn't have a drug enforcement K-9, she bet they knew the signal.

"Checking around to see if anyone knows anything about the drugs we found in a cowboy's truck yesterday."

"I heard about that. I can't believe he did it," she said.

"He didn't," Tyler said from behind her.

"So you haven't noticed anything suspicious? No strangers wandering around, no one fiddling with a truck door?"

She shook her head.

Tyler remained silent.

"If you think of anything, give us a call, all right?"

The deputy handed her a business card.

"I'm leaving. I'm due in Colorado Springs tonight. I didn't see anything," Susannah said again.

The officer nodded and looked at Tyler. "And you, sir?"

"I haven't seen anyone working on trucks or

trailers here."

"Let us know if you think of anything."

He handed Tyler a card and then the two men moved on.

Susannah held her breath as she watched them walk away. When they began talking with another cowboy, she let it out and turned to look at Tyler.

"I'm out of here," she said. "Thank you for your help. Please get that Knight guy to find out what's going on. In the meantime, I'll feel like I'm driving a load of TNT."

"Just be careful. I'll catch up to you in Colorado Springs."

"Okay."

She loaded her mare into the trailer and picked up a couple of lead lines hanging from the hook on the back. Tossing them into the storage compartment, she was ready.

Tyler stood by the truck scanning the area.

"That's not any more subtle than what I was doing," she said with a smile.

Now that she was leaving, she felt a bit safer. As long as there were no incidents along the way, she should be good until Colorado Springs. But she'd be afraid of discovery every mile of the way.

He opened the door for her. "Drive safely."

Once Susannah pulled out of the field, Tyler headed for his own truck. Looking up the number for the Knight Agency, he hoped they worked Sundays–or at least had a way to get in contact with them on a Sunday.

"Knight Agency," a female voice answered.

"Is Jesse Knight there?" Tyler asked.

"He's not working today. Can I take a message for him?"

He thought he heard a laugh in the background.

"I need him to give me a call. Tell him it's about drugs at the rodeo."

"Okay, drugs at the rodeo. And who shall I say–"

"This is Knight. Who's this and what about drugs at the rodeo?" a strong male voice said.

"This is Tyler Fallon, is this Jesse?"

"No, his brother Michael. We work together. What about drugs?"

"I can't talk too freely here but there's a problem and I need your help."

"Call back in a half hour. I'll have Jesse here by then."

The line went dead.

Tyler went to the fairgrounds office to talk to someone about boarding Kyle's horses and parking his trailer. His truck was in the impound lot as evidence.

He caught a break and got everything taken care of quickly.

Hitching his own trailer, he scanned the field for the deputies. The police cars were still near the entrance but he didn't see the two men. Had they moved on to others involved with the rodeo—the concession stands, announcers, office help? Nothing said cowboys were involved.

Except, no one would notice a cowboy wandering around the horse trailers--but they would sure notice an outsider wandering around the trucks.

Once loaded up, he headed to town. A few blocks away from the sheriff's office, he stopped and called the Knight agency again.

Jesse answered at the first ring.

"Tyler, how's it going?"

"Not good."

In a few short sentences he brought Jesse up to speed. Ending with, "So we haven't told law enforcement or anyone. The sheriff considers he has his guy and isn't looking any further. I didn't know what he'd do with Susannah so I sent her on to Colorado Springs."

"I'll meet you both there as soon as I can get there. Sit tight. And don't tell anyone else."

"I'm talking with Kyle. I can't let him sit in that jail cell without some hope."

"Tell him we're on it, but not about Susannah's stash. Let's keep that under wraps at least for the present. Colorado Springs could be their destination. If not, I think they'll be moving it further north. Wonder what they're doing now that one truck's out of the running."

"I'm worried about Kyle."

"We'll do our best to get some more intel about the setup there in Pueblo, while trying to figure their next move. Any problem keeping an eye on Susannah until I get there?"

"No. I'll catch up with her before too long."

"See you as soon as I can get to Colorado Springs," Jesse said.

Tyler continued to the sheriff's office parking his truck and trailer in front of the building.

"Hey man," Kyle said lying on the cot in the cell.

"Hey yourself," Tyler responded.

The deputy opened the cell door and Tyler stepped inside.

Kyle swung around until he was sitting on the cot.

"Guess you're not here to spring me," he said.

"Not yet."

"Yell when you're ready to leave," the deputy said, heading back down the short hallway to the office.

When the door closed behind him, Tyler brought Kyle up to date–except for the drugs in Susannah's truck.

"Do you think it's more wide spread or was I just the lucky one?" Kyle asked.

"Who knows? For a minute this afternoon I thought the sheriff's men would search every truck on the field. But they just wandered through talking with everyone asking if they'd seen anything suspicious."

"And even if somebody knew something, they're not going to talk about it. Time's money and the next rodeo starts on Tuesday. Being a witness would be inconvenient," Kyle said bitterly. "Hell, I wouldn't talk about a crime myself if it was going to hold me back."

"They'd have to let the witnesses go on with their lives," Tyler said.

"Not until they wrung every scrap of information from them by questioning over and over."

"Hang in there. I'm doing all I can," Tyler said, feeling his frustration level rise again.

"I know and I appreciate it. But darn it, this was our best season. We were pulling in some serious money."

"And we will again as soon as you're out. At the arraignment ask for bail again. You don't even have a parking ticket on your record. They can grant bail."

"Not if the judge considers me a flight risk. Not if that sheriff gets his way," Kyle said glumly.

4

Tyler nodded. He didn't have a solid response to that. He needed to find a good lawyer for Kyle who could at least get his friend released on bail. Granted, Kyle didn't live in the area, but he was well known on the rodeo circuit and his home address was a matter of record.

Tyler needed to get his friend out of jail and then the two of them could find out who set him up.

"Hang tight, man. We'll figure something out," Tyler said.

"I'm counting on you," Kyle said.

When Tyler left the jail, he drove to a fast food place where he could park his truck and trailer in the back. While he ate, he scrolled through the on-line websites of attorneys in the town. Too many to know who to choose. Picking one at random, he called. As expected, no one answered. Most attorneys didn't work Sundays. He left a message. Then called another one. Same thing.

Frustrated at not being able to get his friend out today, he gave up. With plans to start calling first thing tomorrow, he finished eating and began the drive to Colorado Springs. The only bright spot in the day was he'd see Susannah soon. What was that old saying—every cloud had a silver lining. If so, Susannah was the silver lining in this situation.

As he drove north he considered who could be trafficking in drugs and using Kyle's truck to move the merchandise. There were some hangers on around the rodeos who didn't compete but still seemed to be at all the events. Were they groupies or should they come under scrutiny?

Then there were the cowboys themselves. He knew how expensive it was to follow the circuit, to pay the entry fees, get feed on the road for horses. If not winning prize money, it was a never-ending drain on finances. Sometimes when they placed, the winnings didn't even cover the entry fees. So who wasn't in the money yet showed up at each event?

Nick Montano was one who came to mind. For the last two years the man had been at almost every rodeo Tyler competed in, yet not once had he placed high enough to win any serious money. Who was bankrolling his entry fees?

Tyler made a mental note to let Jesse Knight know some of the men he though should be looked into. He'd include Devan Perlman in that list. Not that he suspected the man of dealing drugs, but he didn't like him hitting on Susannah.

Frowning, Tyler wondered why he cared. He'd seen her around for the last couple of years. Admired her riding ability. She was easy on the eyes and from her handling the recent events, she had a cool head on her shoulders. But he didn't know anything about her social life except she didn't date rodeo cowboys. She'd made that plain when he'd asked her out. From what he'd seen, she mostly kept to herself. He didn't remember ever seeing her with a guy.

Still, Devan's behavior rubbed him the wrong way.

If nothing else, maybe he could help Susannah fend off other cowboys while they searched for a clue to tell them who was transporting drugs.

The drive took longer than he anticipated. It was almost nine o'clock by the time he turned onto the back lot at the rodeo grounds. Bumping over the uneven ground, he took it slow to minimize the impact on his horses.

He smiled when he saw Susannah waving at him. There was room next to her rig for him to pull right in.

She ran over to his truck and smiled broadly.

"I saved you this spot," she said through the open window.

"I appreciate it. I thought I'd be here earlier."

"Well you should appreciate it. I had to fend off half a dozen other rigs."

Her grin told him she hadn't minded at all.

He turned off the engine and got out of the truck. He caught a glimpse of Devan one row over and on impulse swept Susannah into his arms, nuzzling her neck.

"Play up, your friend Devan's watching."

She encircled his neck and held on for a minute.

"The big reunion scene?" she whispered, laughter in her tone.

"Works for me," Tyler said, slowly releasing her.

He liked the way she felt in his arms. What would it be like to have a girlfriend on the circuit? No one to leave behind when hitting the different rodeos. Someone glad to see him even if they'd only been apart for a few hours. Someone to plan a future together.

She smiled tentatively. "You really think this is necessary?" she whispered.

"Hey, no one will think anything of us together if we're a couple. But trying to find out about the drugs on our own might make someone suspicious. We don't know who's watching."

"That's just creepy. Did you eat?" she asked.

"Naw. I wanted to get the horses settled first. You?"

"Not yet. Though I was beginning to think you weren't coming."

"We'll find somewhere to eat in a few. Let me get these guys settled," he said, walking to the back of the trailer and lowering the ramp.

"I can help," she said, joining him.

When his horses had been fed and watered, Tyler got his papers from the cab of the truck. "Guess I'll find the office and let them know I won't be in any events but the calf roping."

"I've been thinking. If you want to try it, I could be your hazer on steer wrestling. I couldn't help in team roping, I'd flub that for sure. But I'm pretty sure I can keep my horse running straight for the bulldogging."

He thought about it for a minute. "Thanks, I appreciate that."

She nodded. "It'll cement our relationship, don't you think?" she asked glancing over at Devan who still stared at them. "That man won't give up!"

Tyler slung his arm across her shoulders and turned her away.

"Ignore him. We'll go to the office together and request the substitution."

"I wish I could lasso a calf, I'd help out there, too, if I could," she said as they walked on the uneven ground.

"Don't worry about it. Kyle might get out soon."

"When they find the bad guy. Then you should sue him for lost prize money."

Tyler laughed. "Like how much would that be? There's no guarantee of winning each time."

"Well, I'd say tell him you would have won every time, calculate the money from that."

"Any money the guy has will be from drugs, so probably confiscated. It's the breaks of the game," Tyler said.

Once they'd squared things with the rodeo coordinator, Tyler suggested dinner. Leaving Radar with the horses, they headed to the outskirts of town.

They found a small restaurant near the rodeo grounds. It was half full of other cowboys lingering over coffee, the remains of their meals plainly seen.

Once their dinner was ordered, Tyler glanced around to make sure no one close enough to hear them was paying any attention. He leaned forward.

"Jesse Knight will be here soon." he said softly. "He suggested we leave things as they are for now. My guess is he'll set up some kind of surveillance to see if anyone tries to get to your truck."

She nodded slowly. "Okay—as long as some local sheriff doesn't come searching and find that stash." She toyed with her silverware. "I'm still worried, though. It's scary to think this thing goes on and normally we don't even know about it. Why would anyone use my truck?"

"Or why Kyle's? My guess is expediency. Maybe it's where you parked. Maybe it's he knows how to remove the panel of that brand of truck faster than any other make. Who knows what he's thinking? And you might not be the only one. He could have stuff stashed in other trucks, too. Trucks he could easily get to unseen."

"It had to be this morning. Radar didn't alert before. It wasn't there before I went to the practice arena. Then I was gone for my event, then I watched yours. It's the only time I wasn't around it."

"Maybe what they had in Kyle's truck was only part of the shipment but the accident had them change plans at the last minute. So they looked for another truck with easy access. Who knows?" he said.

He reached out and covered her hand.

"We'll find out and make sure this kind of thing doesn't happen again."

She studied their linked hands for a moment, then met his gaze.

"I'm glad if I'm in this situation, you're here to help," she said slowly.

Tyler gave her a slow grin. "Me, too."

Gently his thumb began tracing patterns on the back of her hand. "So, Susannah Davis, tell me all about you. If we're involved, I should know more about you than you're a terrific barrel racer and have a dog and red is your favorite color."

"I'm from Bootstrap Ranch in Cody. Do you know it?"

He shook his head.

"It's a place for foster kids. My mother died when I was ten. I never knew my father—he took off before I was born. Bootstrap's a working cattle ranch open to a bunch of foster kids. We were like a big family—rules and regulations, chores to learn, but we also learned to ride. Walt and Sherry are the owners and they encourage kids to be all we can be."

"Did they stake you to that sweet mare you have?" he asked.

She shook her head.

"I saved up and Walt helped me pick her out. Unlike many other places for foster kids, once I turned eighteen, I wasn't kicked out. And then they started paying me for the work I did. Once I had enough money saved, I bought Missy. Walt helped me train her. I still spend most holidays there."

"They sound like really great folks."

"They're amazing. Everyone there loves them. And I can keep in touch with other kids even when they move on. What about you? Where did you grow up?" she asked.

"On a ranch near Wildcat Creek. Funny we're both from Wyoming. My granddad owned the spread for many years, turned it over to my father a couple of years ago. Now he and my brothers run the place."

"So you grew up on a cattle ranch, too. How many brothers?"

"There are five of us. We've all worked on the

ranch since we could ride."

"Did any of your brothers ever rodeo?"

"A couple, but mostly local events. None ever tried for the big prize. My dad's not a fan of my recent life choices. He says it's too dangerous. Bucking bronc and bull riding are, that's for certain. But not what I do."

She laughed.

Tyler watched, entranced by how pretty she was when she laughed.

"Like wrestling a steer isn't dangerous? The act of leaping off a running horse is crazy."

She shook her head and met his gaze, her eyes sparkling.

"Cowboys are crazy," she said.

He shrugged and gave her a slow smile. "It's something to do for now."

"For now?"

"It's a young man's sport. I might have a couple of more years, but after that, there will be others coming up that'll do better."

"But fun while it lasts," she said slowly.

"I think so. You must, too. Isn't this your second year on the circuit?"

"Third, but I didn't compete that much the first year I tried it. It's expensive and I have to fund everything myself."

"Yeah, I hear that. My dad helped when I was starting. But I pull my own weight now. If I make it to the nationals, I'm sure the whole crew will come to Vegas for the event."

Their server arrived with dinner and Tyler reluctantly released her hand.

He dated. He and Kyle often took out local girls who came on to them at the various rodeos. But he didn't hold hands. And didn't spend much time wondering about them. An evening out dancing or dinner and he was back getting ready for the next event.

If someone had told him a couple of days ago that he'd be holding hands with a pretty girl today, he'd have thought him loco. But it had felt good, connected.

Conversation turned back to their experiences with the rodeo. He'd been riding longer than Susannah, still it was fun to hear her take. A bit different, and less wild, than his version.

When they finished eating, he asked if she wanted to head back or walk around for a bit.

"I'd like a walk. After sitting so long in the truck for the drive here, I'd relish some exercise," she said.

It seemed natural when they left the diner for him to reach for her hand again. When she looked at him with a question in her expression.

"Got to play the part, right?" he said with a grin.

"Right, like the hug when you arrived."

"Should I have given you a kiss?" he asked whimsically.

"A hug was fine."

He wondered what it would be like to kiss her? To hold her close to him, feel her warmth, touch that silky hair, kiss her until they were both breathless.

He suspected she'd deck him if he tried. Unless he convinced her it was part of their cover.

"It's not a problem with Radar—your being gone longer?" he asked.

"He's in the horse trailer. I left the side door open, but closed the ramp. He'll be fine there and go with me when I go to the motel."

"You staying at the Starlight?" Tyler asked, naming the nearest motel to the rodeo grounds.

"Yes, you?"

"I have reservations, but I'm thinking now I might hang out in my truck. Depends on what Jesse says when he gets here."

"Oh, I forgot he was coming in tonight. Should

we head back? What if he's already there waiting for us?" she said, stopping.

"He'll call if he gets there and we aren't around. It wouldn't hurt to return, though. What would your dog do if someone messed with your truck?"

"Probably attack. I hadn't thought about that. So that narrows the time when someone could have put the drugs in. When I'm competing, I lock him in the trailer. It doesn't get hot like the truck, and he won't be wandering around looking for me. That had to be the time they put the drugs in."

It was almost midnight when Jesse Knight pulled into the grounds. He recognized Tyler's rig from the description Tyler had given him and stopped behind the trailer.

Tyler and Susannah were sitting in lawn chairs between their two trucks.

"Hey, man. You made good time," Tyler said, quickly crossing the short distance to greet Jesse.

"Not much traffic the later it got."

"You brought your horse?" Tyler asked.

"Two of them, actually Part of the cover. I thought I'd sub for Kyle. Best way to keep suspicions at bay."

"Good idea. You want to park and come back or we'll follow you."

"Follow me. I want a spot near the perimeter if I can find one. Less foot traffic or the possibility of people overhearing."

"We'll be along."

Jesse continued to the far end of the field.

"Let's go tell him all we know," Tyler said returning to Susannah.

She rose and called Radar. They walked toward the perimeter, passing horse trailers and trucks. Horses were hitched to makeshift rails or back of trailers. Some were hobbled but stayed by their owners. For those in the money, stalls were available or a large corral.

Susannah stumbled on the uneven ground and Tyler quickly put his arm around her waist, steadying her.

"You okay?"

"It's hard to see now that it's so dark."

"Hold on to me and we'll be there in no time," he said, glad of the excuse to hold her.

She slowed a bit and took her steps more carefully, but didn't step away.

By the time they reached Jesse's spot he'd unloaded his horses and hitched them to the back of the trailer. Already on top of the trailer he was forking hay from a loft section for them to eat. Tyler introduced Susannah and then asked,

"Need any help?"

"I'll need water. Where's the nearest spigot?"

"About four trailers back. I'll get it," Tyler said, snatching up two buckets.

When the horses were taken care of, Jesse motioned them on the far side of the trailer. He pulled three folding chairs from the storage compartment of the trailer and set them on the ground.

Radar hadn't made a sound, but watched constantly.

"Nice dog. Friendly?"

"He can be," Susannah said.

She reached for Jesse's hand and looked at Radar.

"Friend," she said.

The dog wagged his tail and then went to sit beside Tyler.

She looked at Tyler.

"That's a first. He usually waits for me to sit so he can sit beside me."

"Hey, animals like me."

"Umm." She took the seat next to Tyler.

Jesse took the third.

"Will he warn us if anyone comes close?" he asked.

"Probably," she said.

"Tell me what you know," Jesse said.

The next few minutes were spent discussing all the information Tyler had. Jesse asked questions a few times to clarify things, but mostly listened.

"And no idea of who could be involved?" he asked at the end.

Tyler and Susannah shook their heads.

"I can give you a list of men I wouldn't mind it being, but we don't have a shred of proof for anyone," Tyler said.

"You never know. Something's telling you these men are off a bit. Call it instinct. Who are they?"

Tyler gave him the list of cowboys he'd thought about on the drive.

"I'll have the office check them out. Interesting about that Nick guy. It's not cheap to follow the circuit–especially if there're no winnings."

"His trailer and truck are fairly new," Susannah said. "I hadn't thought about the expense. Good catch," she told Tyler.

Jesse watched them for a minute. "You two involved?"

Tyler and Susannah looked at each other then at Jesse.

"We're using that as our cover," Tyler explained.

Jesse laughed. "Good. First thing in the morning, you and I'll head for the office to get me listed as a substitute for Kyle. By then I might have some more information on the names you gave me."

He rose. "I'm bushed after the drive here. See you around seven?"

Tyler and Susannah rose, too. Radar came to his feet and walked to Susannah.

"See you then," Tyler said. "I appreciate your coming."

"Hey, our family has a strong vested interest in the rodeo. I'm like you, I don't want the image tarnished by drugs. It's a clean competitive sport and I'll do all I can to keep it that way."

5

Tyler walked with Susannah back to her truck. "You heading back to town now?" he asked.

"Yeah. Should I be back here at seven?"

"No need. I'll fill you in when you get here. Have a good night."

"You, too," she said, opening her truck door and giving Radar the command to load up.

The dog gave a sniff at the door and jumped right in afterward.

"He doesn't understand why I'm not doing something when he alerts. I hope I'm not ruining him," she said.

"Naw, I think he knows something's going on. And he's alerted you, so that part's good."

"Well, good night," she said.

"Aren't you forgetting something?" Tyler

asked, stepping closer.

It was dark, many of the others had already gone to wherever they were staying. Others were dossed down in their rigs.

"What?"

Playing a charade had its advantages, he thought, taking her into his arms and kissing her.

He took his time, loving the feel of her in his arms just as he'd imagined.

She responded quickly and heated his blood. He wasn't sure how long the kiss would have lasted if Radar hadn't whined.

"Playing a part?" she whispered when they ended the kiss.

"You never know who's watching," he whispered back.

"Like they could see anything in the dark," she murmured, her arms still around his neck, his still around her waist.

"That was for show. This isn't," he said, pulling her closer and kissing her again.

Susannah felt the kiss to her toes. When he pulled back, she leaned against her truck afraid her knees wouldn't hold her.

"Well, goodnight, then," she said. Was that breathy voice hers? She cleared her throat. "I'll see you tomorrow."

She gave a wave as she pulled away. Her heart was pounding and all she could think about was that kiss. She needed to watch herself around Tyler. He was attractive, fun to be with, and wow—could he kiss!

Driving the short distance to the motel her mind replayed his words–This isn't for show. What exactly did he mean?

She avoided dating anyone on the rodeo circuit after Pete. She had her list of wants for her perfect mate and footloose and fancy free cowboys didn't even make the list.

Not that stopped her heart from pounding from the kiss. It had been unlike any other she'd ever had. For a moment she wanted to forget the rodeo, forget her stupid vow and see where being with Tyler would lead.

Don't go there, she admonished herself. No fantasies about Tyler Fallon. He was fun, good looking and a star athlete, but not for her.

It was for show.

Mostly.

When Susannah pulled into the parking lot, it was half full. Her room was at the far end of the building around the corner. That part of the parking lot was virtually empty. She was rooming with two other barrel racers. It was late but she had her room key. She hoped she wouldn't wake them—or find herself being questioned as to why she was so late.

She locked up her truck, took Radar for one last walk and went to the room. She was the last to arrive. Her roommates were both sound asleep.

Quietly she took a quick shower glad for the down time. Fearful she'd give something away if she relaxed her guard, she liked being alone for however long she had.

"Hey, you're coming in late," Maggie Potter said sleepily when Susannah left the bathroom, leaving the door ajar so she had some light in the bedroom.

"It's not that late," she said, hoping Maggie didn't look at the clock.

No such luck.

"It's after midnight. You out with that hot Tyler Fallon?"

She pushed herself into a sitting position.

"We went to dinner–"

"Anything going on we should know about?" Maggie whispered with a teasing grin.

Before Susannah could reply, Maggie grinned. "If that blush is anything to go by, there's lots I should know about."

"We had a nice dinner," Susannah said primly.

Maggie laughed quietly. "So spill. Tyler Fallon doesn't usually mingle with other competitors on the rodeo–preferring to share his favors with buckle bunnies from what I hear. So I definitely want the deets."

Susannah didn't usually share confidences with the other women on the circuit. Yet, would it enhance their cover to make up something to convince them they were a couple and not question why they spent time together? Not that she expected the drug dealer to be one of the women she knew. But then, she didn't expect it to be any of the cowboys she knew either.

Peggy sat up and switched on the light. "What's going on?"

Maggie grinned at her. "Sorry if we woke you. Susannah's been out carousing with Tyler Fallon."

"Dinner," Susannah protested. "To celebrate our winning today," she improvised quickly.

"Congratulations on winning today. You rocked," Peggy said.

"Thanks. It's mostly because of my horse."

"I don't know, I have a great horse and I didn't even finish in the top five."

"Practice helps," Susannah said.

She'd watched Peggy ride and sensed a hesitation on the turns. "If you need any coaching, I'd be glad to spot you at practice one day to see if I can give you any pointers."

Peggy smiled. "That'd be great. This is my first time away from my home-town rodeo and it's a lot tougher than I expected."

Susannah nodded. Only the top contenders stayed with the circuit. Expenses were usually the reason people dropped out before the end.

But the lure of Las Vegas for the granddaddy of rodeos was the strongest draw there was. She finished fifth in the nationals last year. This year she was higher in the ranking heading toward Vegas. Maybe she had a shot at finishing in the top third. Of course the dream was finishing first--in the big money.

Maggie looked at Susannah with a teasing grin. "Still waiting to hear about your dinner with Tyler. No going to bed until we hear everything!"

Susannah turned off the bathroom light and went to the bed that was hers. She sat on the edge and looked at them with a grin.

"There isn't much to tell. We went to dinner, came back to the parking area, met up with an old friend of his, then I came here."

"Who's his old friend?"

"Jesse Knight."

"The famous bull rider?" Maggie asked.

Susannah nodded. "Yes, apparently he and Tyler go way back."

Actually she had the idea Tyler knew of Jesse only because of his relation to the rodeo and his investigative services. She was glad Maggie only knew of Jesse's rodeo history.

"Wow, what's he doing here?"

"He's going to sub for Kyle until that situation gets cleared up," Susannah said, glad she had a ready answer.

Maggie's expression became solemn. "Do you think Kyle was really smuggling drugs?"

"No, I don't." Susannah was definite.

"Some people are saying Tyler's in on it, too. I don't want to think that, he's so hot. But how could he not know his partner was smuggling drugs?" Peggy asked.

"Kyle wasn't smuggling drugs, someone planted it in his truck."

Maggie shrugged. "I'm sure that's what he's saying."

Susannah hadn't expected others to believe Kyle was guilty. She knew he wasn't, but couldn't explain why. Would that be the reaction of everyone if the drugs in her truck were discovered? People would think she was smuggling? The sooner she got rid of the packets, the better she'd feel.

"Anyway the cops took Tyler's truck apart and there was no evidence of drugs anywhere," Susannah defended. "I believe him that Kyle's innocent."

Maggie looked at Radar, lying beside the bed.

"Does your police dog track drugs?"

Susannah nodded.

"Maybe he should check out all the cowboys, see if any have it on their hands or something. He could tell right?" Maggie asked.

"He could."

She didn't want to give any indication that she'd already done that. They'd walked by every truck on the grounds and the only one Radar alerted on was hers. And two cowboys she'd encountered. But that could be from smoking pot, legal in Colorado.

The guilty party would have been careful in handling drugs. It probably wasn't out of the plastic the entire time he had it. Would there be any trace on a cowboy for Radar to alert?

"We can go together and flirt with all the guys. They'll never suspect," Maggie said gaily.

"That's an excuse to flirt with everyone," Peggy said dryly.

"We're going to be investigators to see if we can find anyone dealing drugs, if flirting is our cover, what's the harm?" Maggie replied.

"No one on the circuit would be so dumb, would they?" the younger woman asked.

"What about Kyle? He got busted in Pueblo when they found drugs in his truck."

"I heard about some cowboy. I didn't know him." She looked at Susannah. "Do you know him?"

"Only to say hey to."

"But Tyler Fallon is Kyle's partner and now he and our Susannah are an item," Maggie said, bouncing up and down on the bed. "Spill, girl."

"I told you already. We went to dinner, came back to the camp and met up with an old friend of his."

"Who happens to be a world champion bull rider, but she skims over that part," Maggie interposed.

"Is he single?" Peggy asked.

"Who?" Susannah asked.

"The world champion?"

"He's married, I think. I don't know for sure.

But I don't think he's interested in seeing anyone."

The last thing she wanted was Peggy or Maggie making a play for Jesse and impeding his investigation.

"But Tyler's single and hot. And took Susannah out. She never dates cowboys, so this is really special," Maggie said.

Peggy looked impressed.

"We're getting to the good part, aren't we?" Maggie asked, focused on Susannah. "Did he kiss you good night."

Did he! Like she'd never been kissed before. But she wasn't going to let anyone know that.

"Oh, he must have, look at her rosy cheeks," Peggy said. She laughed. "Now I want the details."

"Yes he kissed me goodnight and I came here. End of date."

"How many times?" Maggie asked. "Did he curl your toes?"

Susannah laughed, totally embarrassed. She tried to appear nonchalant about the kisses, but her heart began pounding in remembrance.

"Of course he did," Peggy said. "I know which guy he is and he'd curl my toes if he kissed me."

"So when are you going out again?" Maggie asked.

"I don't know."

Maggie looked at Peggy. "We need to keep an eye on her."

Peggy nodded. "So tell me how we're investigating for drugs. Shouldn't cops be doing that?"

Maggie told her about Radar and her idea to visit all the cowboys.

"That'll be a job. There're so many," Peggy said.

"Which will make it fun."

"Except–what happens if Radar identifies one," Peggy asked.

Maggie looked at Susannah and then Peggy.

"That's when we leave it to the cops. We'll tell them what we found and let them handle it."

"Good plan."

Once the lights were out Susannah lay in the dark wondering how Tyler and Jesse would view Maggie's crazy scheme. Her only hope was they wouldn't find any cowboys at all using drugs.

6

The next morning Susannah headed for the rodeo grounds early. She wanted to feed Missy and exercise her to free up her day. It was a rest day for them. The rodeo in Colorado Springs started Tuesday. But to keep her horse in top shape, she'd ride the arena and practice turns. She hoped she was first in practice.

And then she wanted to find Tyler and tell him about Maggie's crazy idea.

Despite the early hour, many cowboys were already up and their horses were being fed and groomed. A few were already in the practice ring warming up or in the main arena going through their paces.

She fed and watered Missy. Tyler's two horses had already been taken care of. He and Jesse must have already met up and gone off.

She didn't know how good Jesse was with team roping, but hoped the all around cowboy would be an asset to Tyler. And truth to tell, she was a bit relieved not to ride as hazer for the steer wrestling event. While she was sure she and Missy could handle it, a wild steer who veered into her horse could injure her mare. She couldn't afford to have anything happen to her.

"Good morning, you're up early," Tyler said behind her.

When she turned around he gave her a quick kiss on the cheek.

"Good morning," she replied already feeling flustered. She glanced around. There were enough cowboys in the vicinity who looked their way. That was probably the reason he kissed her. It meant nothing, part of the charade.

But to her it meant a lot. She glanced at him and then away, hoping he didn't see how much she liked his affection.

Jesse stood on one side looking amused.

"I guess you two got the substitution set up," she said, reminding herself again the display was for any on-lookers. Was whoever stashed the drugs in her truck among the nearby cowboys? It'd make sense, they'd want to keep an eye on their stuff.

"Yep. Which gives Jesse a legit reason to prowl around," Tyler said

"Speaking of that, one of my roommates from last night suggested we go around and speak with all the cowboys with Radar at our side to see if any have handled drugs."

"You didn't tell them you'd already tried that?" Tyler asked.

"No. Besides, Maggie isn't looking for trucks, she wanted to visit cowboys."

"You stay in a motel in town?" Jesse asked.

She nodded and gave the name.

He looked at Tyler. "How about you and Kyle? Do you usually stay at a motel or hang out with your horses?"

"Depends. At a motel every other stop, to get a shower and a good night's sleep. As long as we know the horses are safe. Other times we just doss down by the trailer."

Jesse looked thoughtful.

"So Kyle's truck was sometimes parked at a motel. That'd be a better place to stash drugs than here where there're people milling around all the time."

"So it might not be a rodeo cowboy involved?"

Susannah asked.

"I don't know for sure. It could be concession-aires, officials who travel with the circuit, any one of a lot of people," Jesse said. "I'm still waiting for some feedback on the names I called into the office last night. Until I get that, there's not a lot to do. I'll work my horses to get the kinks out and then Tyler and I'll practice. It's been a while since I've done any roping."

Susannah watched as he walked away.

"Is Jesse any good for heading and heeling?" she asked.

"We'll find out, won't we?" Tyler gave her a grin. "See you later."

Peggy was waiting in the main arena when Susannah entered riding Missy. She rode over to her.

"I'm taking you up on your offer," Peggy said. "If that's still okay? I got one of the cowboys to put up the barrels. And the cowboys riding around said they'd stay at the perimeter."

"Okay. Let's start before anyone else comes in. Show me."

Susannah rode to the finish line to watch Peggy.

Peggy headed for the first barrel. Susannah again saw her hesitation, how she'd turn her horse wide.

Peggy did the same thing on barrel two and three, winding up for the finish and rode straight until she passed Susannah, then she pulled up and trotted back. "What do you think?" she asked, stopping beside Susannah.

"I think you're awfully timid on the turns. Don't you trust your horse?"

Peggy patted the gelding's neck. "Of course I do."

"Then turn him sharper on the left turn, practice almost having your foot on the barrel. And don't swing so wide on the right. Same thing. Tight turn. Do it slowly at first then speed up each pass. Then really urge him to give it all he's got on the home stretch."

Peggy took a deep breath and nodded. She practiced three circuits, turning tighter against the barrels at a slow speed, getting herself and the horse used to being so close to the barrel. Then she said she was going for real. She started beside Susannah and she and her horse rode like crazy. They finished faster than Susannah had ever seen her do before.

"Better. I'd practice both those moves over and over until you're both comfortable with the tight turns," she gave as a final suggestion.

"Thanks." Peggy patted her horse's neck. "I saw

you with Tyler this morning. You two look good together."

Susannah smiled, knowing she had a part to play, but wishing she could tell someone what was going on. Maybe get some feedback on if she was totally crazy or not.

"See you later," Peggy said and began riding the configuration again.

Susannah kept Missy on the outer perimeter of the ring and took the horse through the gaits to warm her up. Once Peggy was finished, she'd do a couple of runs. Practice did make perfect and she wanted to make sure her horse was in top shape.

Tyler stood at the gate and watched the women exercise their horses. It looked as if Susannah had given the other barrel racer some suggestions to improve her performance. And the woman had taken them to heart if he was any judge. Her time looked better already.

Mostly, however, he watched Susannah. He loved seeing how she moved with her horse, almost as one. Graceful and pretty, she was a treat to watch.

What would happen when the investigation was over? Would they still be friends? He suddenly wanted to know more about her stance on rodeo cowboys. How could she be so adamant about not dating one when she was around them all the time? Seemed like to him that would give them a lot in common.

He thought about the kisses last night. It felt good to hold her in his arms. And her response showed she wasn't indifferent to him.

He'd stayed clear of dating anyone seriously. Often he and Kyle went dancing with some girls that flocked to the rodeo. It didn't mean anything but a fun night out.

He wasn't going to be on the circuit forever. If they made the winnings this year, he and Kyle would be too caught up in making a going concern of a new ranch to leave it for the time it took to ride in rodeos. Unless they were close to home, of course. Maybe one or two a year for a while just to keep in practice.

What about Susannah? They'd talked briefly about their pasts last night, but she'd never said what she wanted in the future. She was living in the moment with her barrel racing. What did she see for her future? More rodeos? When she stopped making the money, then what?

A question every cowboy asked himself.

He pushed away from the rail and headed back to his horses. He'd take what he could get with

Susannah and hope when the drug dealer was found, they'd continue seeing each other. He felt more than just a cowboy playing a charade. How much more it was too early to tell.

When Susannah had enough, she rode Missy back to the trailer, unsaddled her and replenished her water bucket. Letting Radar out of the trailer, she fussed over him for a couple of minutes before brushing her horse. She was finishing up with the mane when Tyler came around the back of the trailer.

"Want to get something to eat?" he asked. "A few of the concession stands are open today for us that are here."

"Sure," she said. "Can Radar come with us?"

"Of course."

They headed for the midway on the other side of the arena where the concession stands were. Tyler reached out and took her hand. It felt right and not just for show to whoever might be watching.

He glanced at her. She looked straight ahead, her dog walking right at her side. Radar wasn't even wearing a leash.

"Did you and Maggie check out the cowboys?" he asked.

She grinned at that and glanced at him. "No. She slept in late this morning. One of her other friends took care of her horse. She'll be here soon, so it's still a possibility later."

"And if Radar alerts then what will you two do?"

"Call the cops," she said promptly.

"That might be dangerous if the guy suspects what's going on. And if he's involved dealing drugs, you can be sure he knows about drug enforcement dogs."

"We always say 'he' but I suppose it could be a woman involved," she mused.

"Maybe. So what's your choice, hot dogs, pulled pork sandwiches, tri tips?" Tyler reeled off some of the different food offered at the different concessions.

"I want a corn dog," Susannah said with a smile. "And soda and chips and all the junk food I can get for this meal."

Tyler laughed.

"Good thing you're young," he said. "That sounds like a heart-attack on a plate."

"Hey a corn dog once in a while isn't going to hurt. And I'll get corn chips because corn is a grain."

He laughed at that. "Yeah, a really healthy

version of it, too. Come on, there's no line."

Once they both had corn dogs, drinks and a bag of chips to share, they went to the rows of picnic tables and sat at the end of one. It was still early for lunch, so the area was sparsely occupied.

"Thanks," Susannah said as she sat and put her drink down. "I really don't eat like this all the time. Sometimes I even make a lunch if we're a few days at an arena and have a motel room with a mini kitchen."

"And what do you make?"

She looked at him. "PBJ, of course."

He grimaced.

Once again she laughed. Tyler loved hearing the sound. It was infectious and he involuntarily smiled in response.

"Tuna, cold cuts if we have a mini fridge. Usually my roommates go in on the cost so we all eat on the cheap for a while."

He nodded. "Money can get tight."

"This year's been good to me, so far I'm coming out way ahead. Even for all the events I've already paid for, I've made more then expenses."

"You think about Las Vegas?" he asked.

"Who doesn't if they're serious about rodeo. Maybe this year. But if not, there's always next year."

He nodded. "I was hoping for this year. If I

can't get Kyle out soon, that'll be the end of that."

"For the team roping and maybe even steer wrestling. But your score's high on the calf roping and that's a solo event."

"I know. I might have a shot at that. The money's not as big as for the others."

"Money matches risk. If you were a bull rider, you could make a lot more."

"Yeah or get killed. I did bronc riding my first year, busted my leg on the next to last rodeo, so decided I liked showing off other aspects of ranching like roping and steer wrestling rather than staying on a fool wild bronc for eight seconds."

"I think steer wrestling is dangerous. I can't get over the jumping off a full running horse."

He ate another bite and than asked, "What are you going to do in the off season?"

"Go back to Bootstrap and help out. It's the closest thing to a home I have and they can always use the help."

"Is the pay good?"

"No, but the feeling of paying it forward is. I get room and board for me and my animals, so I'm satisfied."

"And what do you plan to do with your winnings?"

"Unlike you, I don't ever expect to own a ranch, though I have a pretty good idea how to run one from working with Walt and Sherry. I don't know. When I get tired of the rodeo, or get too old, maybe I'll hire on somewhere. I like Texas," she said slowly.

Looking at him she wrinkled her nose.

"But that's years away. For now I love competing, love the different towns, love the camaraderie of all the participants and the folks connected with rodeo. Even the crowds and especially the applause."

Tyler suspected she had years of competing in front of her. She couldn't be that old and her mare was young. She'd only improve with practice. He just hoped she didn't get injured. His broken leg had put him out of the money that year.

The talk turned to Texas and where she'd been and what she'd liked.

Tyler enjoyed talking with her. She was easy to be around. And she didn't flirt.

Which set her apart from most of the women he dated when on the circuit.

Would they ever have had lunch together if not for the situation with the drugs? Probably not. She tried to keep her private life separate from the rodeo.

Now that he was getting to know her better, he was glad circumstances threw them together. She was pretty, friendly, and kind. Not all people associated with the rodeo were. Many were cut-throat competitors doing all they could to get ahead.

"I need to get back to my horse," she said a few minutes later. "And meet up with Maggie."

He glanced at his watch. Time had slipped away.

"I'm going to see if Jesse's found out anything," Tyler said, rising when Susannah did.

They walked back to their rigs. Maggie was sitting on the tailgate of Susannah's truck.

"Hi," she said hopping off. She smiled at Tyler.

Susannah made introductions conscious of Tyler holding her hand, his fingers linked with hers. She knew exactly the image he projected and felt flattered. Even knowing it was a charade she felt special and cherished.

"You two stay out of trouble," he warned with a twinkle in his eye. Giving Susannah a quick kiss on her cheek, he headed for the perimeter of the field.

"Wow, he's even better looking up close," Maggie said, watching him walk away. "Girl, you're winning more than barrel races this year!"

"Maybe. You want to walk around now?"

"Yeah, might as well. Then I've got to exercise my horse. It's hot now, so I don't mind waiting," Maggie said, reluctantly turning away from watching Tyler.

"Do you have a plan or are we just walking up to every cowboy in the place and shaking hands like we're the welcome committee or something?" Susannah asked.

"I've been thinking about it. We need a gimmick. I thought maybe we could be collecting donations for Kyle's defense."

Susannah stared at her for a moment. "From the rumblings I've heard, a lot of the cowboys think he's guilty."

"So we give them something else to think about. I scrounged a old coffee tin from a restaurant in town. We can use that," Maggie said. She resettled her cowboy hat and nodded when Susannah said,

"Well, that'll make it so official."

She smiled at Maggie. She slapped her leg for Radar.

"Okay, here goes nothing. Radar, heel."

The two girls wandered around stopping to chat with the other contestants. Maggie had memorized everyone's stats it seemed. She had something to say to each cowboy showing she knew more than Susannah expected–or the cowboys—about scores, horses and plans.

It was flattering and more than one cowboy flirted right back at her.

Susannah began to feel like a fifth wheel.

As they headed for another trailer, she looked at Maggie. "You don't need me."

"Sure I do, you don't think I'm this forthcoming on my own. It's part of the act to see what we can find out. But I have to say I'm getting discouraged. Your dog hasn't paid any attention to anyone."

"That's good news, isn't it?" Susannah said. "I hate to think anyone I know is involved with drugs."

"Maybe, but doesn't help get Tyler's partner free," Maggie said.

"We haven't even covered half the lot, let's keep going. How do you remember all those stats?" Susannah asked.

"I have a great memory. Never know when I might want to chat up some cowboy. It pays to know something about them," she replied with a wink.

7

Tyler found Jesse sitting in the sliver of shade by his trailer, working on a laptop.

"Anything?" he asked.

Jesse shook his head. "Still waiting for more intel. I'm expanding the search parameters to include those who follow the circuit but who aren't involved as contestants. For all we know the smuggling operation has nothing to do with the rodeo, just some smart operators taking advantage of the traveling most contestants do."

Tyler sat in the empty chair next to him.

"Where's Susannah?" Jesse asked, glancing around and then looking at Tyler.

"She and a friend are wandering around to meet all the cowboys. They're taking Radar in hope he'll alert for drugs."

Jesse shook his head. "And if he does?"

"They say they'll call the cops."

"Unless the guy is wise to drug dogs and know he's been made. No telling how far someone would go to escape detection."

Tyler nodded. "Still, with all the people milling around, it's unlikely he'll do anything overt, right?"

"From your lips," Jesse said, closing the laptop. "Let's get in some practice. It's been a while since I roped anything, much less a running calf."

Three hours later Susannah and Maggie plopped on their beds in the motel.

"I'm more tired than if I'd competed a dozen times today," Maggie said, eyes closed.

"Me, too." Then Susannah laughed. "So far we only identified two guys and they were smoking pot when we approached them." She reached over the side of the bed and petted Radar. "You did good, boy."

"So much for my brilliant idea," Maggie said.

"Well, all's not lost, remember Brian Dougherty, he wanted to get to know you better."

"As if I'd become involved with a rodeo cowboy. Unlike you, I'm staying clear of guys whose first love is chasing the buckle."

"I'm the same way," Susannah said lazily. A

quick nap wouldn't hurt anything.

"Except for super hottie Tyler Fallon."

Her eyes flashed open. She'd forgotten their charade.

"Well, he's different," she said.

"Yeah, he's a winner, good looking and he seems head over heels for you. What's not to like?"

"If he and Kyle win enough money this year, they plan to buy a ranch and settle down."

"Ah, perfect timing for forging family ties. When's the wedding?"

Susannah was silent for a moment thinking about what it would be like to be courted for real, to marry Tyler, a man who understood her own aspirations on the rodeo circuit. Who spoke her language so to speak. She loved Walt and Sherry on the Bootstap Ranch, but to have a place of her own, a home to raise kids in. It was something she rarely dreamed about.

"Did you fall asleep?" Maggie asked softly.

Susannah closed her eyes and feigned sleep. It saved having to respond to the question.

A knock on the door woke Susannah up. She rolled over and looked at the clock. It was after six! She had actually fallen asleep.

Maggie stumbled from her bed and opened the

door. "Oh, it's you," she said, and turned around to flop on the bed again.

Tyler stood in the frame, smiling at the picture in front of him as Radar came over, his tail wagging.

Susannah rose and crossed to the door. "Is something wrong?"

"No, I wanted to see if you wanted to get supper. I didn't know this is how you spend your afternoons, I thought you two were going to track down some suspects."

She rubbed her face, trying to become fully awake.

"We found a couple of cowboys smoking pot, but since that's legal in Colorado, we didn't consider that a lead. No one suspicious after that."

"So, supper?" he asked.

"Yes, come on in. I just need to splash some water on my face and redo my hair."

Tyler stepped into the motel room. Maggie had dragged a pillow over her head.

"Want to join us?" he asked the recumbent form.

"Thanks but no. I want to go back to sleep," she mumbled from beneath the pillow.

In a short time, Susannah was ready to go.

"I need to see to the horses and feed Radar and

then we can go," she said as she grabbed her purse.

"Feed mine, too, please," Maggie's muffled voice said.

"Will do."

"I'll leave my truck here and we'll take yours, if that's okay," Tyler said, heading to the bright red pickup. "I want to keep it under supervision if we can."

"Works for me. Did Jesse find out anything?"

"Nothing definitive. He'll join us for supper. We practiced today and he's checking in with the agency while I pick you up."

They hurried through the chores until all animals had been fed.

"Shall I leave Radar here?" Susannah asked when Tyler said it was time to let Jesse know they were ready.

"Might as well. It'd be cooler than sitting in the truck in some parking lot while we eat."

After dinner had been ordered, Jesse leaned back in his chair. The family-style restaurant they'd chosen was only half full. Families with small kids seemed to dominate the clientele. None sat near them, so after a quick glance around, Jesse relayed what he'd learned so far.

"So basically nothing," Tyler said when he finished.

"We'll move all those to the bottom of the list of possibles." He glanced at Susannah. "You're cleared, too."

She blinked.

Tyler took exception. "You can't have suspected her!"

"I take nothing for granted. But her record's spotless. I think that's one reason they chose her truck. Whether in addition to Kyle's or after his truck was out of commission, I don't know."

"I guess I feel good about that,"

Susannah wasn't so sure. She was touched Tyler jumped to her defense so quickly.

Looking at him, she tried to remember they were only playing a charade to fool anyone watching them. Sometimes, it was hard to remember.

"You hear from Kyle?" Jesse asked.

"I called the jail this afternoon, bail was denied—flight risk. I tried two lawyers, too, but only one wanted to touch the case. It seems open and shut to them, so he was talking plea bargain and I hung up on him. Do you know anyone?" Tyler asked.

"I know a couple in the state who have done some work for us. Let me see what I can do," Jesse said. He looked at both of them. "And the drugs won't be in your truck much longer. I contacted some DEA guys, they'll be here tomorrow. We'll meet away from the rodeo and they'll take possession of the drugs."

"That'll be a relief," Susannah said wholeheartedly.

Tyler and Susannah drove Jesse back to the trailers. After double checking on all the horses, they got Radar and headed back to the motel.

"Do you think the drugs are still in the door?" Susannah asked, when Tyler parked close to the car in the next slot.

"I do, and I figure we'll make it as hard as possible for anyone to get to them tonight. We don't know how far they want to chance using your truck," he said, shutting off the engine. He turned and looked at her. "You doing okay?" he asked.

She nodded. "Except for living in fear some cop will find the drugs and think I'm smuggling."

"A few more hours, hang in there. Once the DEA agents take the drugs, you can relax about being found out by cops. Then we just have to keep watch to see who tries to take the panel off."

Susannah looked at him in the faint light.

"Unless we have some sort of round-the-clock surveillance, we might never catch him. Who knows when or where he makes the switch?"

"I figure once the drugs are gone, we make it tempting for him. We'll spend a night or two at the fairgrounds. With Radar's help, we can watch and be prepared. If not here, then maybe the next town, or the next."

"I hope we can catch this guy," Susannah muttered.

"Me, too. For Kyle's sake if nothing else."

"And before too much more rodeo time is lost," she said. "In the meantime, what else can we do?"

"Act normal. There's a place in town one of the guys told me that has dancing. Want to go tomorrow night?"

She tilted her head slightly. "Part of the charade?"

He reached for her hand, lacing his fingers through hers.

"More of a date, I'd say."

Susannah's heart skipped a beat. "So not part of the charade."

He slowly shook his head, his gaze searching hers for some clue as to her feelings.

Slowly she smiled. "I'd like that a lot," she said.

Once in bed that night, Susannah was a long

time falling asleep. She kept thinking about Tyler, the feelings that were growing around him, and her long-time vow to avoid rodeo cowboys.

The next day was the first day of a three day rodeo in Colorado Springs. The synergy of the fairgrounds was electric. Horses were being groomed. Others were working out to get them limbered for their event. Cowboys milled around, ignoring those who had come to watch and get a preview of the cowboys and their horses by wandering around the vast parking area.

Susannah loved the feel of the rodeo. The air of excitement, the fans, the adrenaline rush when her event was up. Even Missy seemed in high spirits. For a few hours, she'd forget the quest to find the drug smuggler and focus on the rodeo.

Peggy rode up, her horse practically dancing with energy.

"Thanks for your help, I've been practicing," she said, leaning forward to pat the horse's neck. "I feel really lucky today."

"Go for it. I hope it helps," Susannah said, mounting Missy and walking along with Peggy as they headed for the staging area prior to their event.

Maggie was already there walking her horse in figure eights. She smiled and waved.

"I heard Peggy's going to give us a run for our money today," she called when they were close.

"I'm shooting for first," Peggy said, looking nervous but determined.

"Good luck!" Maggie said. "But I think I'm going to beat the socks off everyone here."

The others laughed.

Susannah hadn't known these women for very long, but they were already friends. While each wanted to win, she knew she wouldn't be too unhappy if Maggie or Peggy placed ahead of her— this one time. She was focused on getting to the national event in Las Vegas in the fall. One or two second place wins wouldn't kill that chance.

She drew number six. Fingers crossed that was a lucky number.

Tyler rode into the group of women, heading straight for Susannah.

"Good luck, today," he said, drawing up next to her.

"Thanks. You, too. You and Jesse are in all three events?"

"Yep. Win, lose or draw, I sure appreciate his subbing for Kyle."

The grandstand announcer called the next event—the barrel races.

Tyler reached over and caught Susannah behind her neck, drawing her closer for his kiss.

"For luck," he said gazing into her eyes.

Heart racing, she smiled. "For you, too," she said leaning over and brushing her lips against his.

Then it was time for concentration, not fantasies about a hot rodeo cowboy who was helping her find who was using her truck for contraband.

She didn't forget their date that night. And her heart skipped another beat. She grinned at the teasing from the other barrel racers and settled herself in the saddle to focus on the event.

Tyler rode to the side of the arena where he could see a little over the high fence but was out of the way of the contestants. Jesse joined him a couple of minutes later.

"Watching the barrel races?" he asked, following Tyler's gaze.

He nodded.

Jesse glanced around and noticed they were away from others.

"I don't want anyone to see the DEA agents, so after the events, you and Susannah want to meet us in a secure location? We'll do the drug exchange. They want to substitute harmless packets with a tracking device to see if they can follow to the next stage. These drugs are bound for somewhere."

'No problem. Just let us know when," Tyler said.

Susannah was next and when she and Missy started the run, Tyler silently urged them on. Flying past the first barrel, it tipped slightly then righted. He held his breath as they almost spun on a dime around the second barrel and headed for the third. Once around they flew back to the starting point and finished the run with the highest score of the event.

"She's good," Jesse said.

"Yep. Let's hope we do as well."

One event followed another. Tyler focused on psyching himself to do the best he could at each event. When the team roping event came, it turned out Jesse was almost as good as Kyle. They came in third, but almost tied the second place team.

On the steer wrestling, they came in second. The points went to the total for the finals. Susannah watched from the end gate as he performed in each event. She caught her breath when he jumped off his horse to wrestle that steer to the ground. She'd never get use to any cowboy doing that. When he came in among the top two she cheered louder than anyone else.

He came in first in calf roping--and made his personal best time for this year.

"That was fabulous!" Susannah greeted him when he had remounted his horse and rode out of the arena.

"Could have been better," he said, though he was pleased with the result.

"Always. Still, you're tops right now."

"Two more days to go on this rodeo, who knows what could happen," he replied.

They drifted toward the horse trailers, letting the horses cool off as they walked.

"Jesse wants to meet off site," Tyler said. "We'll take care of the horses and then head out."

"Finally," she said. "I don't want to end up like Kyle. How's he doing?"

"Hanging in there. I've filled him in on what's going down. If we could prove someone else is doing this, he'd be out in a heartbeat." Tyler fisted one hand and pounded his thigh. "We're so helpless until this plays out."

"It will. Then you two can rack up all the points needed to make it to the finals," she said.

"Where you'll be yourself if you keep on winning," he said.

8

Susannah pulled out of the rodeo grounds and turned left as Jesse had instructed. It took a good twenty minutes to reach the ranch and turn onto the drive. Cattle grazed in a field to the left of the long drive. It must have been half a mile in before she glimpsed the house and out buildings. Following Jesse's instructions, she drove straight to the barn and parked.

A man rested one foot on the lower rail of the corral as he watched the few horses dozing in the afternoon sun. He watched Susannah drive up and when she got out of the truck, he turned and walked her way. Radar leaped down and sat beside her.

"Help you?" he asked.

"I'm Susannah Davis. Is this your place?"

"No." He narrowed his eyes. "Are you here to

see the owner?"

"Depends," she hedged, turning to close the door to the truck.

When he took a step closer to the truck, Radar gave a low growl which stopped the man instantly.

He looked at the big German Shepard. "Not too friendly, is he?"

"Only when he wants to be," she replied.

He still hadn't given her any information. Was he Jesse Knight's contact?

He backed up a step, keeping his eye on the dog.

Another man came around the corner of the barn.

"That's the woman," he said. He stayed back when Radar turned his attention to him. "We're the good guys, but until that dog knows that, I'm not coming closer. DEA Agents Bennett and Sampson. Jesse coming?"

She nodded. "He should be right behind me."

Even as she said it, the big black pickup truck pulled into the yard. Jesse and Tyler climbed out and walked toward Susannah.

"Dirk, good to see you again," Jesse said with a smile, holding out his hand.

"Interesting situation you're in," Dirk said gripping his hand.

"You've met Susannah, this is Tyler Fallon. His partner's in jail in Pueblo. Suspected of drug smuggling. Same set up as we have here. If her dog hadn't alerted us to the drugs chances are good they'd have gotten away with it."

"The dog's a drug dog?"

"Used to be," Susannah said. "He's retired on disability, but nothing wrong with his nose."

Susannah called Radar away from the truck. The two DEA agents had come prepared with tools and made quick work of removing the panel. The drug packets were still sandwiched in between the struts of the door. Removing them, Agent Sampson opened one and sniffed.

"Seems like," he said, closing it up. He put a tag on it with his name and date. Each packet was logged into evidence and then all were put in a metal carrying container.

"What if the crooks come for the drugs and find it's gone. Won't they be after Susannah?" Tyler asked.

Dirk nodded. "Which is why we've come prepared. We needed to know how this looked, but it's pretty standard. We have packets of powder sugar that will match close enough. We've installed tracing devices in several of them. We're hoping it'll fool them long enough for us to close in."

Susannah felt relief that the drugs were no longer in her door–and that the DEA didn't believe she was transporting. Tyler leaned against the back of her truck beside her watching the men work.

"Can they call the sheriff in Pueblo and get Kyle out?" she asked.

"Not yet. I asked Jesse the same thing. For all they know, Kyle is involved. Nothing so far has cleared him. Besides, they don't want to spook whoever's involved with this. Kyle showing up cleared of any wrong-doing would be a huge red flag. Whoever's doing this has to be connected with the rodeo. So they're taking no chances."

"That makes sense, but it's too bad for Kyle. It could be days before they find the guy."

"I know. I can't even send him word for fear of tipping them off."

Susannah watched the men packing the powder sugar into similar bags. Who could have accessed her truck? And where?

"Jesse's really mad about the whole thing," Tyler said a moment later. "He and his family started the WRA years and years ago. They still have strong ties to the rodeo and he feels personally attacked."

"I think any honest cowboy would be outraged," she said.

Radar watched the proceedings. He had alerted again when they opened the door panels then watched as the drugs were placed in the metal container. Then he relaxed, but kept watch on what was going on.

She smiled at Jesse. "I already feel ten times lighter. I hated knowing it was there. And hate thinking about some crook getting it to sell. Kids could be involved and there's nothing lower than some guy preying on kids."

"You're right. We'll catch him, Susannah, it's just a matter of time."

"I hope it's sooner rather than later," Tyler added.

"So we don't need to keep up our charade," she said slowly.

Tyler looked at her. "Of course we do. We change nothing that might give a hint we're on to them. It's not so bad, is it?"

She shook her head, hoping the warmth in her cheeks didn't show. "It's tolerable," she said, lying her teeth off.

She was growing unexpectedly interested in this cowboy. To continue their charade for a while longer suited her just fine.

Repacking the door with the sugar, the DEA agents spoke with Jesse and then called a thanks to Susannah and Tyler.

The two men walked behind the barn and in a moment a nondescript black sedan drove down the drive.

"Where are the people who own this place?" Susannah asked, realizing no one had come out of the house the entire time. Wouldn't the owners be curious as to what was going on?

"In town. Apparently this place has been used for meetings before where the DEA wants to keep it away from prying eyes." Jesse shrugged. "Works I guess."

"The plan now?" Tyler asked, pushing away from the pickup truck.

"We wait and watch, same as before. But this way if things don't go the way we want, we're not letting drugs hit the market."

"And Susannah?"

"Keep her close. The hope is they'll take the stash and move on before they realize it isn't the real deal."

"And not come back to ask her where it is?" Tyler said sarcastically.

"Yeah, well, there's that possibility, which is why you two need to be joined at the hip until we get these guys. However, I suspect they're going to think long and hard before approaching her with Radar always at her side."

"Okay, then, Susannah, consider us joined at the hip."

She'd never had a boyfriend on the circuit and even though this would all end once the crooks had been caught, she'd enjoyed the ride as long as she could. It might prove to be more fun than she expected.

"We drive back separately, right?"

She wasn't sure she was as confident of her safety with the drugs gone as she'd hoped to be. She knew there were no drugs, but the bad guy didn't. As far as he was concerned, his stash was safely in her truck door.

"We'll follow right behind you. When we get near the rodeo grounds, we'll hang back at the entrance for a little while. I don't expect any action today or tonight. My guess is Loveland is their target site. One of my brothers is meeting us there. More eyes on the truck that way," Jesse said.

Susannah drove back to the rodeo grounds, trying to think when her truck was left alone for people to mess with it. Her best guess was at the motels she stayed in. From bedtime to next morning it sat in the parking lots unattended in most cases even by surveillance cameras.

Maybe she should pick motels that had surveillance cameras from now on. They were probably more pricey, but if it deterred smuggling, she was all for it.

Arriving back at the rodeo grounds, she fed her horse and walked her around a little bit before retying her by the trailer. They had one more event tonight and then she'd be going to the dance with Tyler.

Despite telling herself over and over it was part of their charade, she couldn't help being excited. A fun night of dancing and swapping stories with others was just what she needed to get her mind off the situation.

And she got to spend more time with Tyler.

As if thinking about him conjured him up, he and Jesse drove in. Jesse dropped him at his rig and continued.

"How was your day?" Susannah called. She refused to glance around to see if anyone was close enough to overhear, but wanted to pretend they hadn't spent most of it together.

He walked over. "Good, and yours?" Leaning in, he brushed his lips across hers. "I missed you," he said.

Her heart skipped a beat. For a moment she wished it was true.

Then reality returned.

"Me too," she said, reaching out to brush her fingertips across his shoulders.

He captured her hand and brought it to his lips, kissing the palm and folding her fingers over to keep in the kiss.

"You ready for tonight?'

"My race or the dance?"

"Both."

"Yes. I think Missy's in fine shape and I'm looking forward to the dance."

She hoped he attributed her enthusiasm to their cover, yet she truly meant it. She liked being part of a couple--sharing their day, talking about their pasts, finding common interests. Even his plans for the future were something to dream about.

"Are you ready for the team roping again?" she asked as he held her hand, they walked to where his horses dozed in the late afternoon sun.

"As we'll ever be. Jesse's gone to practice until our event. He needs no practice hazing the steer in that contest."

"He was a champion, doesn't he still feel the urge to compete?" she asked.

"I didn't ask. I think he's too tied up with this investigation agency to follow the circuit. And my guess is he doesn't need the money from one or two rodeos. The big bucks are in Vegas. And he won there big time."

"Maybe." Susannah sat on one of the stools as he took care of his horses.

"Are we taking my truck tonight or yours?" she asked at one point.

"We'll take mine. Jesse said he'd watch Radar and your truck."

"I think the best time to mess with anyone's truck is in the wee small hours when they're parked at motels along the way. No one's around. Here anyone could get up in the night because they can't sleep or some cowboy comes back for a drunken binge at the local bar," she said thoughtfully.

"You may be right. Jesse and I discussed that. Which is why we wanted to leave your truck here overnight. I can drop you at the motel after the dance and pick you up in the morning."

"Okay. But what of Radar?"

"He can spend the night with me."

She considered it. "He's my protector, too, you know, not just my pet."

"Or we can swing by here before I take you to the motel," Tyler amended smoothly.

She nodded. "I'd feel better. What if this is the drop point and they show up at the motel and my truck's not there. I definitely want Radar with me."

"If that happens, they'll look around for the truck, not storm your room."

"Does that mean you're staying with the horses again?"

"Not a hardship. Anything to catch these guys and get Kyle out of jail."

She nodded, feeling deflated. Tyler was doing this for his partner. She needed to keep that at the forefront.

"Jesse told me they'd finished the background checks on as many of the cowboys as they could get intel. As expected the majority live from event to event, winning some, losing some. No one has a huge influx of cash unaccounted for. He couldn't find out much on Nick Montano, though. His office is still trying," Tyler said softly.

"So no clear cut winner for the suspect of the year award," she said.

"I also threw out a couple of others--two of the

concessionaires follow the circuit. I've seen their trucks in Pueblo and here—the corn-dog guy and the one selling tri-tips. Jesse said he'd check them, too," Tyler added.

He'd have thought if either of them was involved, they'd find the same hiding place in their own truck doors, why use others?

Unless the shipment was so large one truck doors wouldn't hold it all.

Or it could be Nick Montano who had no source of money he could tell. Tyler wished the Knight Investigation Agency had access to bank records like cops did. Still, they'd amassed a lot of data that he hoped would help them narrow the suspects.

"We'll keep an eye out to see when someone tried to access the door."

The last thing he wanted was for some crook to come after Susannah if he realized the substituted packets weren't his. Catching him in the act would be the best plan.

At the evening rodeo event, the crowd was much larger than the afternoon event. Once again the excitement was almost palatable. Susannah came in a close second to Maggie's first place. And Peggy squeaked into third place by a half second.

She was so pumped Susannah laughed, glad her pointers had helped, sharing in her delight at finally placing in the event.

"I've created a monster," she said after she congratulated Peggy. "I need to watch myself or you'll be passing me up."

"I can't believe I came in third. Susannah, thank you so much for those pointers. We've been practicing every moment we can." She petted her horse on the neck. "He did good, didn't he?"

"So did his rider," Susannah said with a grin.

She took Missy back and rubbed her down, giving her a handful of carrots as a treat when she fed her. Checking around her area, she put Radar in the truck with the windows rolled down all the way. It was still warm, but with the windows completely down, the night breeze wafted through keeping the interior the same temperature as outside.

"Stay," she commanded. She leaned in, "And don't let the bad guy in," she whispered giving him a hug.

Heading for the arena she hoped she was in time to see Tyler and Jesse perform.

It was crowded, but she squeezed into a small area that had a pretty good view of the arena and watched as the calves were released and then the cowboys rushed out trying to beat the time for getting the calf.

Tyler finished top in the steer wrestling. Susannah knew she'd never get used to him leaping off his horse to wrestle those steers to the ground. Her heart was in her throat when he made his move.

Whoa, she thought, blinking as the feelings slammed into her. She was getting too caught up with Tyler. Their alliance was a charade to catch the bad guy

She tried to tell herself that she'd be as concerned for any other cowboy who did the steer wrestling, but it wasn't true. She watched Devan and while she hoped he wouldn't get hurt, she didn't have that heart-stopping worry that he'd be injured. He did well in the event, but not number one.

She pushed her way through the crowd and walked back to her truck. She couldn't be falling for Tyler. She had vowed never to become involved with another rodeo cowboy. They were lots of fun, sexy, a bit arrogant, and super athletes. But they also had little staying power. They rode the high of winning with all the perks that came with it— including a girl in every town.

Radar barked in happiness to see her.

"I know, I should have stayed when I brought

Missy back," she said opening the truck door to let the dog out. "I need to remember we're not truly involved."

"Involved with what?" Nick Montano walked by, looking at Susannah and Radar.

"Hi Nick."

She glanced around. There were few people around. The focus was on the arena and the competitions going on.

"Not riding?" she asked, glad Radar was beside her.

"Finished for the night. You done?"

Susannah nodded.

"Heading for the motel?" he asked.

"Actually Tyler and I are going dancing when his events are over."

"Where?"

"Some cowboy bar in town."

"Maybe I'll see you there. You two taking Tyler's truck?"

She was instantly alert. Was he fishing to see if her truck was going to stay here?

"Probably. I'll leave Radar here with my horse. Dogs don't fit in cowboy bars."

"Good idea. He's a good watch dog. Must make you feel safe."

"He does," she said, reaching out her hand to place it on her dog's neck. This was the longest conversation she'd ever had with Nick. Was he being friendly or was there more to it?

"Have fun. See ya," he said, walking down the line of trucks and trailers.

Susannah watched him, wondering if he was the man behind the drugs.

When Tyler rode up some time later, she was sitting in a camp chair, gazing off into space, trying to decide if Nick's questions meant anything.

She smiled at him. "How'd you do?" she asked.

"Came in second on the steer wrestling last guy beat my time by a split second. Zero time on the team roping event, first on calf roping."

"Your best bet for the finals in Las Vegas," she said.

"Unless I can get Kyle out of jail and we score big as a team." He dismounted and walked closer. "I wish this would come to an end here. Every day Kyle's in jail is lost money for us, not to mention agonizing for him. And makes it harder to acquire the needed points to make the finals."

"Could we force the issue? Say something about the car's window not opening all the way so I'm going to take it into a shop? That would spook him, don't you think?" she suggested, rising to walk with him toward his own horse trailer.

"Sure, but who would we tell?"

"Everyone we suspect," she said. Without being asked, when he'd removed the saddle, she began brushing his horse on the opposite side from Tyler.

Together they made short work of the task, while she told him about Nick's unexpected visit. Then Tyler fed the gelding and took him to the make-shift corral with his other horses.

"It's not a bad idea," Tyler said at last. "We'll run it by Jesse in the morning. Now a quick stop at the motel to freshen up and we're heading for some serious dancing."

"I'm all for that. For a while I want to totally forget the you-know-what and have fun."

When they reached the cowboy bar an hour later, it was jammed. Susannah recognized some of cowboys from the rodeo. Those she didn't recognize she figured were locals. She and Tyler found a small table near the far right. The four-member band was pumping out fast music while the dance floor was full of people having a great time.

They ordered and then Tyler rose and held out

his hand. "Ready?"

Susannah joined him and soon they were dancing to the beat. When the song ended, another cowboy asked her to dance. Tyler shrugged and put her hand in the other man's. He stepped to the sidelines trying to fight the feeling that rose.

Susannah was not his girlfriend.

What if she were? Then he'd stop any man in the place from dancing with her. He wanted her undivided attention.

Pathetic. She agreed to help with the investigation by playing a role. She'd mentioned early on that she didn't date rodeo cowboys. He'd heard rumors about a bad breakup a couple of years ago with another cowboy. He wasn't on the tour this year.

He watched as she danced with the man. Ambling back to their table, he saw their drinks had arrived. He sat and took a long swallow. Two minutes later the song ended and Susannah came back to the table.

"You didn't want to dance with someone else?" she asked, sitting down and taking a swallow of her drink.

"I came to dance with you," he said easily.

She looked at him. "Then why so agreeable to

hand me over to that other guy?"

He studied her a moment. Was she annoyed? Were her expectations to dance with him all night? Slowly he smiled, staring into her eyes.

"So you'll appreciate being with me all that much more, of course."

She burst out laughing.

"Right. Just so we're clear, I'm here with you and if you don't want to dance, we don't dance."

He took a long drink, slammed the bottle down and rose. "Then let's dance."

They danced almost every dance after that. Susannah had a great time. Her favorites were, unexpectedly, the slow dances. She relished being held in Tyler's arms. Loved the way he snugged them right up together, moving in time to the rhythm of the ballads. She'd close her eyes and wish the moments would last forever.

Finally it was time to leave.

"I've had fun," she said as they walked out to Tyler's truck.

"I'm glad. I did, too," he said.

Opening the passenger-side door for her, he leaned in and kissed her. His eyes studied hers when he pulled back, and to his surprise, she leaned forward and gave him a kiss.

He wanted to say something. To tell her the evening had been special. That he was more interested in her than as a partner in a charade designed to fool others. He felt there was some connection between them, that maybe they should see where that led.

But he wasn't sure how she'd react. And for Kyle's sake, he needed to ride this through to the end.

He pulled back and closed her door, going around the truck to the driver's door. He wanted the perpetrator caught, Kyle released, and to get back on track to make it to the nationals.

And then he was going to lay his cards on the table with Susannah Davis. He wanted her in his life. He wanted her to be a part of his life now and in the future.

9

They had one more day for the rodeo in Colorado Springs. Then it was on to Loveland. When Susannah arrived at the rodeo grounds, she was ready to instigate her plan.

Tyler had fed his horses and was already working one out in the practice arena. Susannah fed Missy and groomed her. She wanted her to be on top form for their event today.

When she thought about finding the person responsible she became even more determined.

Then the thought of the charade they were playing would end made her wish to let it go on for just a little longer.

She loved being with Tyler. Being part of a couple. Sharing ideas and plans, enjoying each other's company. Even when sitting by the horse trailers as night fell. They didn't have to do things all the time for her to like being with him.

Yet she had to remember it was all for show. He'd never said anything to suggest he'd want to keep this relationship going. And what of her vow never to get involved again with a rodeo cowboy?

Tyler was different, she argued with herself.

She'd thought Pete was faithful until she found out otherwise. She'd only known Tyler for a few days.

Not true, she'd seen him on the circuit last year and this year. She knew his reputation as a straight shooter. He showed loyalty to his friend Kyle, and had the same values of honesty and integrity she had..

Sighing, she finished grooming the horse. She needed to concentrate on her event today. And their plan to see if talking about replacing the truck window spooked the culprit and had him try to retrieve the drugs tonight.

When Tyler joined her a few minutes later, she smiled, trying to keep her heart from pounding in anticipation of spending time with him.

He dismounted and she went to help him brush the horse when the saddle was removed.

"I'm ready to start project fool-the-bad guy,"

she said softly so only he'd hear.

"And how do you propose to do that?" he asked.

"I thought all night and came up with a brilliant plan," she said, grinning at him across the horse's back. "We'll walk around all the suspects while I'm fiddling with my phone. You'll ask me what I'm doing and I'll say trying to find an auto shop that will fix my window tomorrow before I head for Loveland. I'm sure that'd get someone's attention."

"Worth a shot. I haven't told Jesse yet."

"Time enough if we can get the word to all who are suspects. Then we watch the truck tonight and catch him in the act."

When they turned the horse into the make-shift corral, they started on the plan.

Ambling along, when they were close to Devan's spot, Tyler asked what she was doing. Giving her answer, Susannah glanced at Devan. He was soaping some leather to keep it supple. He glanced up as they walked by, so Susannah knew he'd heard. Was he the one?

They walked up one side of the row of trucks and trailers and down the other.

At the end of the second row, Tyler stopped and glanced behind them.

"You don't think it's odd that we're just walking up and down the rows?" he asked. "I'd find that suspicious."

"We'll say I'm trying for a good signal," she replied "We only have a couple of more to go."

"Let's get it done. I'm not sure it's really going to work," Tyler said.

She shrugged and headed for the third row. "Maybe not, but I still think it's worth a shot. And we're almost done. We'll finish soon so we can get something to eat and be ready for the afternoon events."

When they reached the concession stands a short time later, Susannah suggested, "One of us get a corn dog and the other the tri-tips so I can talk about the window at each one."

By the time the afternoon events were starting Susannah was satisfied they'd let everyone they suspected know the car was heading into the shop the next day.

"The only problem I see," Tyler said as they saddled their horses, "Is that perp could be someone we never suspected. Then they still don't know of the possibility of the door being taken apart."

"Then we're no worse off than right now," she

said, disappointment flaring. She hoped one of the men who'd over heard her was the culprit.

Only time would tell.

"I want to keep watch tonight. You and Jesse don't get all the good stuff."

Tyler laughed. "Yeah, right, good stuff—take down a drug dealer. It could be dangerous. There's a lot of money riding on those drugs."

"Maybe I should have Maggie take Radar to the motel tonight. Even with the possibility of losing the drugs if discovered, the guy might not try anything with him around."

"Or put him in the horse trailer early on so the guy can't see him, but ready to let him out if the guy takes the bait. Radar might not be in top form to still be on active duty, but I know he'd know how to take the guy down if he runs."

She nodded, a feeling of anticipation building. They might have their answer before tomorrow morning. She looked at Tyler.

And she might have her answer on that front as well.

"It'd be great if we get the guy before we leave here. Kyle's spent too much time in jail for something he didn't do," Tyler said.

"I know. Let's hope tonight's the night."

When the rodeo began, Susannah focused on her riding, on sharp turns and pushing Missy for all she was worth at the last stretch. They finished with Susannah's personal best this season. And came in first place two seconds ahead of second place. She hoped the rest of the day went as well.

As if being keyed up was the means to success, Tyler and Jesse nailed first place in the team roping and Tyler came in first in steer wrestling and a close second in the calf roping.

The three of them went to dinner together at a family-style restaurant near the fairgrounds. There were plenty of people from the rodeo so they didn't discuss the situation, though Tyler had brought Jesse up to speed on their plan.

He shook his head. "I'll be amazed if that works."

"It's a long shot," Susannah agreed. "But we had to do something. This waiting is stretching my nerves beyond my limit."

"Not to mention Kyle's," Tyler added.

"Right. This has to end sometime, why not sooner rather than later?" Susannah said.

"Yet you left your truck at the fairgrounds," Jesse said when the waitress placed their orders on the table.

"No one's going to do anything while it's daylight, do you think?" Tyler asked, digging into his burger and fries. "We figured it would look more natural for us to take my truck."

Jesse shrugged. "Probably is. You realize you may not have given the clue where the real crook was. We only suspect some of these guys, without much else to go on, how can we narrow down to one?"

"My money's on Nick," Susannah said. She pushed a french fry into the ketchup and popped it into her mouth. The tantalizing milkshake was near to hand, but she wanted to eat something before losing herself in the delicious ice creamy delight.

"Mine's on Devan," Tyler murmured. "He and Kyle don't get on and I bet he figured stashing the stuff there would be payback if it was discovered—which it was. I wish that guy had never run the red light. If not for the accident—" He stopped. "Actually, I guess that was a blessing in disguise. Now we know what's going on and can stop it."

Jesse nodded. "And I'm wondering if we should encourage a sweep of the parking area again during rodeos with a drug dog. Just to make sure there's not more of this going on. When you did it, the guy could have had his truck somewhere else."

"Or he's stashed more since then," Tyler said.

"A dog will alert on a lot of pot smokers," Susannah said.

"But we might find other stuff too," he said. "First we need to get the guy who stuffed the dope in Kyle and Susannah's trucks," Tyler said. "Here's hoping tonight's the night."

They had the evening events to get through, then the plan could be put in place.

Once again Susannah won her event. If she kept this up, she'd be a shoo-in for the Nationals.

Tyler did well, but neither seemed as concerned with their performance tonight at they were with their plan.

Leaving the truck window part way down to bolster her false claim, Susannah and Radar got in Tyler's truck making a big deal of fitting the dog in the narrow space behind the seats so anyone who was interested could see they were taking off, leaving Susannah's truck beside her trailer.

They drove to the motel where they each had reservations. Checking in, Susannah was sharing again with Maggie and Peggy. Neither was in the room, so she left her duffel bag and slipped out to walk to the ice machine, Radar at her side. Not seeing anyone around, she continued on the outside hallway to Tyler's room.

He was waiting for her. Leaving Radar in his room, they walked to his truck and returned to the fairgrounds. Leaving his truck on the side of the road before the turn to the parking lot, they looked around. It was late enough most of the rodeo contestants who were camping by their trucks had turned in. There was a soft murmur of conversation from a couple of sites, but for the most part it was quiet.

Slowly they circled the perimeter until they reached Jesse's outfit. He was sitting in the dark.

"Ready to move?" Tyler asked.

Jesse rose. "I'm ready. Let's take it slow and watch for anyone who might still be moving around. I talked to my friend at DEA. They're going to be ready to move, but won't enter the parking area unless we call. They don't want to scare the guy away. Sometimes letting the merchandise go is safer than catching the guy. Especially since they have the tracking devices in the packets."

"He's already lost part of this merchandise," Tyler said. "I think he'll go for this and chance it."

"Let's hurry," Susannah whispered.

"No rush. If he's going to act tonight, he'll wait until he thinks everyone is sound asleep. I'd say after midnight."

They crept to Susannah's trailer and slipped inside. Earlier she'd stashed three camp chairs inside so they'd have something to sit on. With the tailgate up, there was only the small side door to give them a view of her truck. Sitting well away from the door made sure no one could see them.

Time seemed to move slowly. Susannah shifted slightly in her chair. She was getting tired of doing nothing but sitting silently in the dark.

Tyler reached out and touched her, finding her hand in the dark and taking it in his.

She liked his touch. She remembered the dancing they'd done. She'd much rather go back to that than be here.

But she didn't feel like they were wasting time. Surely the drug dealer would want his supply before she took the truck to a repair shop.

Checking her watch, it was barely midnight. How much longer?

The minutes passed by slowly. Tyler's thumb rubbed the back of her hand gently, absently. It sparked an awareness of the man that she hadn't expected. He was doing this for Kyle, she told herself again and again. But she was falling for the cowboy and wished things had been different. She couldn't forget she'd refused when he asked her out.

If she'd accepted back then, would things be totally different now?

To while away the time, she let herself think about what it would mean if by some miracle Tyler wanted to continue their relationship after everything was over. Dare she trust a rodeo cowboy again? Not all men were like Pete. She recognized this and wondered if she was cutting herself off from possible happiness by holding to that vow made when she first discovered his perfidy.

If Tyler and Kyle made the nationals and won the prize money, they planned to buy a cattle ranch and leave the rodeo. That would account for the roots she was searching for. She knew something about a cattle ranch thanks to her upbringing on Bootstrap Ranch. She could even help out with the finances if she won prize money in her event. And she and Missy were well on their way to qualify for the finals.

She could envision Tyler coming into the house at the end of each day, tired, but satisfied with the way the ranch was going. They'd have dinner, spend time on a front porch gazing at the land and talking about plans and dreams.

She wanted a home of her own. She wanted roots and ties and a lasting relationship with a man who loved her wholeheartedly. When she sighed, Tyler squeezed her hand slightly as if encouraging her. Wouldn't he be surprised if he knew what she was fantasizing.

There was movement. Susannah almost held her breath. Tyler leaned closer. Jesse went on alert.

The door of the truck opened, the overhead light coming on momentarily, then it went dark.

Susannah gripped Tyler's hand. They could barely make out a dark figure, silhouetted slightly by the pencil-thin flashlight focused on the door.

They could scarcely see him or hear him. If they hadn't been watching, they would have missed it entirely. The guy was good. No wonder he almost got away with it.

A few minutes passed and then the door slowly closed. The man rose and Jesse said, "Now!"

He and Tyler spilled out of the trailer and ran toward the man. Tyler snatched up his rope hanging by the trailer door.

Susannah only a step behind them.

The man heard them and took off, running down the center of the drive.

Tyler stopped and swung his lariat overhead twice then let it fly. It landed squarely across the shoulders of the running man. Yanking hard, Tyler pulled the man off his feet. Jesse reached him in seconds. The man struggled with the rope, but Tyler kept it taut.

"Now I know how my horse feels," he said, pulling on the rope, hand over hand as he drew nearer the man on the ground.

Susannah turned on her powerful flashlight and aimed it at the man's face. He stopped struggling and seemed to give up. Beside him on the dirt drive was a canvas bag, undoubtedly holding the packets he'd taken from the truck.

It was the man who sold corn dogs.

10

The next morning, Susannah was so tired she could hardly see straight. Between the adrenaline rush the night before and not getting to bed until almost five in the morning and getting up at eight, she was dragging.

None of that mattered to her horse and dog. She fed Radar at the motel and then they headed back to the fairgrounds. Once Missy was fed, Susannah would pack up and head for Loveland.

The DEA agents had taken her statement last night. When she driven back to the motel by a uniformed policeman, she'd noted Jesse and Tyler were still at the police station. What time did they make it to bed?

While Missy ate, she leaned against the horse trailer and almost fell asleep on her feet. She wasn't sure she should drive to Loveland quite yet. Maybe another nap would help. No sense risking life and limb on the highway.

Radar was lying on the ground watching her. He turned his head when he heard the black pickup approach. Standing, he wagged his tail.

Susannah smiled when she saw Tyler. He stopped next to her rig and leaped out of the truck. Stopping to pet Radar he approached Susannah. When she stepped forward to meet him, he picked her up with hands at her waist and swung her around. She grabbed his shoulders as they twirled around and around.

"Kyle's free! He was released this morning and is waiting to get his truck and then he'll pick up his horses and meet us in Loveland," Tyler said exuberantly. He set her back on her feet and grinned at her.

Her hands still on her shoulders she grinned back. "That's great. I know both of you are relieved."

"We are."

The minutes ticked by as they gazed into each other's eyes. Slowly Susannah let her hands slip from his shoulders and Tyler dropped his own hands from her waist.

"So did the DEA guys call that sheriff?" Susannah asked, feeling breathless.

"They did. They got a full confession from the corn dog guy as well."

"He has that huge food truck, why did he stash the drugs in other people's trucks?" she asked.

"His food truck is subject to inspection by local health officers at any time. He was afraid they'd discover the drugs, so he's been planting them in other trucks for two years now."

"Wow, he got away with it for two years?"

"On this schedule. Apparently a couple of years ago, he had a different rotation of rodeos and did it then, too. He supplies some guy in Loveland. He named the guy and the DEA was all over it. Jesse was fit to be tied that he used contestants in the WRA for two years."

"But he's been caught, that has to be satisfying for him," Susannah said.

She was beginning to feel self conscious standing so close to Tyler, yearning to touch him again, to have him kiss her, to continue their charade.

"Wait, you said Kyle was joining us in Loveland," she said slowly.

Was it a manner of speaking, or did Tyler want

to actually see if they could become a couple.

Jesse pulled up next to them, his trailer already hooked behind his truck.

"You two take it easy. And good luck at the Nationals. We'll be there rooting for you both," he called from the truck.

"Thanks for all your help," Tyler said going to the open window.

Susannah joined him.

"Hey, I'm glad you called me," Jesse said. "None of us in the family wants this kind of trouble. Glad we caught the guy. He also admitted putting dope in another guy's truck. The cowboy who got injured in Pueblo, so his truck's still in Pueblo and after Kyle's arrest, our friendly dope dealer decided to let it go figuring the guy would be back in the rodeo next year."

"I hope they throw the book at him," Susannah said.

"Me, too," Tyler said.

"I think they plan to. See you in Vegas," Jesse said. With a wave he pulled out.

Tyler turned to Susannah. "Are you heading out now?"

"No, I need to take a nap first. I'm too tired to drive without falling asleep at the wheel."

"I haven't had any sleep, so I'm probably even more a danger. How about we get something to eat and catch a few hours sleep and then head out together?"

"Okay," she said wondering how long this relationship would last.

She wished now that she'd accepted him when he asked her out last year. Who knows where they'd be today?

Tyler slung his arm around her shoulders as they walked back to her horse. Checking to make sure she was taken care of, they took Tyler's truck to the nearby diner. Radar was left safely ensconced in the horse trailer.

When they'd given their order, Tyler took her hand in his.

"We have something to discuss," he said, idly playing with her fingers.

"Oh?"

She felt breathless again. Did he have any idea how he made her feel?

He glanced at her, then looked at their hands. He cleared his throat.

"I think we're good together," he began.

"How so?" she asked. "Play acting in front of rodeo contestants?"

He looked directly at her. "Yeah, that, too. But in lots of other ways. We both love the rodeo, but don't plan to make it our life forever. We both like ranching, we want to build for the future."

She nodded. Where was he going with this?

"You said once you don't date rodeo cowboys," he said.

She nodded again. Her heart began pounding.

"But these last few days haven't been so bad, have they?"

She shook her head. Was he going to ask her out on a real date, not something just to fool anyone watching them?

"I know these last few days were a charade, so we could be together all the time and not raise suspicions. But I was thinking that maybe we could continue, not acting now but for real."

Her eyes widened. "Continue seeing each other you mean?"

He nodded. Then made a wry face.

"Actually, I think I want something more than that."

"Okay, what exactly?" If her heart pounded any more strongly it'd jump out of her chest.

He swallowed. "I was thinking maybe marriage."

Susannah's eyes almost popped out of her head. "What?"

"I know, I know it's way too soon, but I've been aware of you all season. Heck, I wanted to get to know you better last year. I've followed all your runs, saw you with others and wanted to know you better. Now that I do, I think we'd do really well together—on the rodeo circuit and afterward. You know Kyle and I are planning to start ranching in the next year or two, depending on when we can get the money together. My dad will help, too. You have some interest in that as well. You'd make a great rancher. And if you like, we could take in a couple of kids who don't have another home to live with us like those ranchers on Bootstrap Ranch. What do you say?"

Susannah didn't know what to say. She loved this man. But he hadn't mentioned anything about love. Sounded more like a business deal except he'd definitely said the M word.

"I'm making a mess of this, aren't I?" Tyler asked. "What I should have started with is I love you, Susannah. I love everything about you from your silky blond hair, big blue eyes, your figure that won't quit to the way you care for your animals, to your love for adventure, to your stand on right and wrong. I've never loved anyone like this. I think it'll last forever. In fact I'm counting on it."

"It's pretty fast, don't you think?" she asked, her heart racing. It wasn't too fast for her. She'd realized she loved Tyler a day or two ago.

"Maybe, but when you're sure of something, you go for it. And if you say yes, we can have a long engagement, to get to know each other better and all. You don't have to answer now. Think about it. Think about me," he said.

"I've been thinking about you nonstop since we began this charade," she said.

"You have?"

He looked startled, then pleased.

"I have. And I don't need time to think it over any more. I love you, and I'd be thrilled to become your wife."

"Wow." He grinned, rose and pulled her to her feet to wrap her in his arms and kiss her.

The entire diner erupted in applause.

Susannah knew she must be a bright red but she didn't care. Her heart blossomed with love for this rodeo cowboy.

When they sat back down, she smiled at him.

"I don't need a long engagement, but do think we need to concentrate on getting to the nationals and winning some events. If I win any money, then I'll be able to contribute to the ranch as well. If it's to be my home, I want to be a part of it from the get go."

"So a December wedding, then? Right after the finals? Then, with luck riding with us, after the honeymoon we'll start looking for that ranch."

"That sounds perfect to me," she said, reaching out to touch his hand, thrilled when he turned his palm up to hold hers.

"What about Kyle?" she asked.

"What about him?"

"How's he going to take all this?"

"He's fine with it. I told him last night I was going to ask you—if I got up the courage."

She laughed. "A steer wrestler having to garner courage?"

"Well, my future was on the line with your answer. I promise I'll do my best to make sure you'll always be glad you threw in with me. I love you!"

"I love you."

Susannah knew she was throwing caution to the wind to tie her life to a rodeo cowboy's, but this time she was betting on a sure thing.

If you liked A **Cowboy Charade**, you'll love **The Cowboy Next Door**, book 1 in the Cowboy Hero series.

If you enjoyed **Cowboy Charade**, please consider leaving a review.

More books by Barbara McMahon

Cowboys of Wildcat Creek

Valentine's Cowboy Rescue

Shelly and the Cowboy

Kristi's Cowboy Hero

Holly's Reluctant Cowboy

A Cowboy for Eliza

Cowboy Charade

Sweet Reunion Romance Collection

Unexpected Reunion

Unpredictable Reunion

Unanticipated Reunion

The Talmadge Sisters

Letters to Caroline

Michelle's Marriage Deal

Trusting Abby

The Harts of Texas Series

Rebel Heart

Tangled Hearts

Reckless Heart

Cowboy Heroes Series

Blue Bells on the Hill

Cowboy's Bride

One Stubborn Cowboy

Crazy About a Cowboy

Never Doubt a Cowboy

Cowboy Marshal

Summer Cowboy

Second Chance Cowboy

Movie Star Cowboy

Tropical Escape Series

Island Rendezvous

Come into the Sun

Island Paradise

Tropical Escape Series

Island Rendezvous

Come into the Sun

Island Paradise

Rocky Point Series

Rocky Point Legacy

Rocky Point Reunion

Rocky Point Promise

Rocky Point Hero

Rocky Point Inn

Rocky Point Dawn

The Ultimate Billionaires
The Cynical Sheikh
Falling for the Sheikh
A Sheikh of Her Own
The Unforgettable Sheikh

Sweet Romance Stand-alone Collection
Because of You
I'll Take Forever
Jared's Promise
Mail Order Bride
Not Really Married
Sweet Meant To Be
The Cowboy Comes Home
The Paper Marriage
Trusting Jake
The Banished Bride

A Sweet Clean Christmas Romance Collection
The Christmas Cop
The Cowboy's Special Christmas
A Soldier's Christmas
A Teaspoon of Mistletoe
The Christmas Locket
A Key West Christmas